Tales From The Graveyard

Guy N. Smith

SINISTER
HORROR
COMPANY

PRESENTS

GUY N. SMITH

Tales FROM THE GRAVEYARD

Tales from the Graveyard

Edited by J. R. Park
Interior design by J. R. Park
Cover art by Matthew Morris

Published by The Sinister Horror Company

Tales from the Graveyard -- 1st ed.
ISBN 978-1-912578-24-5

SinsiterHorrorCompany.com

This book is dedicated to all my fans over the past forty years.
My sincere thanks for continuing to read my novels.

Contents

Introduction

Back in 1992 Andy Hurst, a GNS fan, launched *Graveyard Rendezvous*, a fanzine devoted to virtually everything concerning my work and lifestyle. It was an in depth look at how I became a professional author and covered my years living on the remote Black Hill in the wilds of South Shropshire.

By the time *Graveyard Rendezvous* saw publication I had written 60 novels starting with *Werewolf by Moonlight* (New English Library) up to *Witchspell* (Zebra USA). The second issue saw the start of the serialization of *Night of the Werewolf* previously only published in Germany by Erich Pabel. In 1976 issue No.3 was a special *Crab*s issue. No 4 introduced *The Black Fedora* and No.5 had *The Old Bride's Column* written regularly thereafter by Jean, my wife, about what GNS had been up to and what it was like living with him!

However, the immense amount of work involved in publishing a regular fanzine was proving difficult for Andy in conjunction with all the other demands on his time so, commencing with issue 6, it was taken over by Black Hill Books in 1995. It then increased in size from 31 to 60 pages and was in A4 format.

From then on *Graveyard Rendezvous* covered a much wider field. This included stories by fans as well as originals by myself, an in depth look at my lifestyle, including our donkeys, goats and feathered stock. I also wrote a long running series on advice to budding writers, *Successful Horror Writing*. This covered devising a plot, suitable characters and the preparation of a detailed synopsis. Only then are you in a position to begin writing the novel. Working from the synopsis, which you will undoubtedly change as the novel progresses, ensures that you will arrive at the correct wordage for the finished book.

Basically, though, *Graveyard Rendezvous* is the ultimate in all types of horror.

Sadly this publication became much smaller with issue 23. This was solely due to advanced technology, primarily the website where all GNS information appeared and a continuation of *Graveyard Rendezvous* would only have been a repetition of this.

However, *Graveyard Rendezvous* lasted up until issue 41 which was published in the summer of 2012. Throughout its lifetime, though, it featured some truly gruesome horror in virtually every field of the genre.

Hence I decided to publish a selection of these stories in book form rather than allow them to disappear into the mists of time. *Tales from the Graveyard* contains stories which I consider to be the most diverse and gruesome to appear in

Graveyard Rendezvous.

Black Hill Books still has a small stock of back issues numbers 7,8,9,11,13,14,15,19,20,21,34,40 & 41. These are available by post at £2.00 each including postage, and can be ordered from www.guynsmith.com *

(*Availability and cost are correct at time of going to print but may change, please check website or get in contact for most up to date information.)

In the meantime, enjoy a good read of the stories within these pages.

Happy Nightmares!

Guy N. Smith

Guy N. Smith

The Shooting on the Moss

(from Graveyard Rendezvous 1)

Guy N. Smith

Evil lurked deep down on the slime.

The glorious twelfth had done it's damnedest to bely tradition, Charles decided as the Range Rover splashed its way down the rutted, muddy track which meandered along the mist enshrouded slopes of the valley from the main road a mile and a half behind. The purple heather had taken on a shade of depressing greyness, visibility was reduced to less than fifty metres. The monotonous whine of the wipers was getting on his nerves, cutting swathes through the opaque film of fast drizzle on the windscreen. Neither he nor Peter had spoken for the last half hour, just muttered curses each time they came to a gate.

And yet another bloody gate! Peter slammed the passenger door shut as he jumped down into a puddle, splattered his new plus-twos, hurried forward to the obstructing barricade, tugged at a rusted bolt, left the gate to swing shut on its grating hinges as the vehicle clattered over the cattle grid. In the back of the Range Rover a Labrador dog whined its impatience. Like its master, it was overweight, lacking regular exercise but the weather had not dampened its enthusiasm.

'We'll never find any grouse in *this*, Charles,' Peter broke the long silence. 'And even if we do, they'll be lost in the mist before we can even get a shot.'

Charles did not reply because there was nothing to add to his companion's logical observation. This was the outcome of a whim which had started in the claustrophobic atmosphere of a stockbroker's London office one afternoon last spring. Nostalgic memories of youthful grouse shooting on a rolling sun-drenched moorland, where you sweltered in shirt sleeves and the scent of the heather was sickly sweet in your nostrils, of coveys of whirring grouse, salvos of gunfire, beaters and pickers up, panting dogs lapping thirstily in a rushing burn. One phone call to Stewart, the land agent in Invernesshire, and it could all become reality again, a return to those halcyon days for Peter and himself.

Just one phone call could bring it all back. It had, and was in the process of destroying it all in a matter of hours. Mankwill wasn't a 'proper' grouse moor, Stewart had pointed that fact out with true Scottish bluntness and honesty at the outset. Just an expanse of moorland inhabited by a flock of scraggy sheep for which the tenant, Macgregor, paid a pittance of a rent. The agent added, with a touch of dour humour, that, 'If it wasnae for the mountains in the way, ye'd be able to see Loch Ness from the Moss!' The sporting rights had never been leased because they, 'were na worth guid money,' but the factor was open to any offers, 'and if ye bag a brace, then ye've got the best o' the bargain!' Two hundred pounds for a three-year lease on two thousand hectares, the offer was accepted within three days, starting from August 12th. And perhaps Macgregor, the crofter, would act as beater and guide for a tenner and the occasional nip from there hip flasks.

And here we bloody well are, Charles thought, two hundred quid for a walk in the mist, every possibility of falling down the mountainside or blundering into a bog, and if we're lucky enough to escape either of those then we'll be back in London by tomorrow night, totally disillusioned. But at least they would have Macgregor to safeguard their welfare, he surely would not spurn the opportunity.

'No-oo,' the ageing shepherd gave the impression of trying to withdraw his sparse and bent frame in the saturated smock that dripped rainwater into the tops of his patched wellingtons. He leaned up against the doorway of the tumbledown farmhouse at the apex of the valley, stared down at the ground. 'No-oo, sir, not for a tenner, not for a *hundred* pounds, would I go up to the Moss wi'ye, neither in mist nor sunshine, summer nor winter. Even the sheep have more sense than that.'

'Why?' Peter asked, and there was a hint of relief in his voice. An excuse, a god-sent escape route from this miserable place; a let off. After all, it had been Charles's idea from the start, he had only gone along with his old school friend in order not to offend him. Peter had not really wanted to go grouse shooting. Back in the city it had seemed a pleasant enough diversion from the stress of an artificial existence; up here, at the mercy of the elements, it wasn't so appealing. All the same he was curious to discover why the flockmaster was refusing to go up to the Moss. And, of course, the raw dampness was responsible for that tiny shiver that began at the base of his spine and goose pimpled its way right up to his scalp.

'Ye've na' heard aboot Ferguson, what happened to him up on the Moss?' Toothless mouth agape with incredulity, those grey eyes now elevated and staring, seeming to shy away from the mist that was creeping down the mountainsides and encircling the tiny farm. 'Ye *din'na* know about Ferguson?'

'We've never even heard of this Ferguson,' Charles spoke with a note of irritation. In fact, we don't give a damn about him, all we're interested in is getting some sort of value for two hundred quid which we've chucked down the drain. All the same, he was unable to suppress a shiver. It was the weather, of course. 'It was during the Great War, I was a wee boy then ma father lived here. Ma mother died at childbirth,' Macgregor had stepped back a pace, clutched the rickety door as if he had a mind to drag it shut and have done with the foreigners from the city. 'Just as ma dear wife did, her baby with her. There was a shortage of meat and the Laird turned a blind eye to anybody who helped himself to a deer or grouse, so long as it was'na too many. Ferguson, he lived over at Cornharrow, just a we holding. One day, a day just like today with the mist covering the mountains he turned up here with his gun. They was pretty near to starvation over at Cornharrow and the deer were all up on the Moss.

'He wanted ma father to go with him to find a beast, so the two of them set off. By late afternoon, there was no sign of them, so I went up the slope as far as the start of the Moss to look for them. I heard a shot. Just one. *And then i heard 'em screaming!'*

Macgregor was inside the house, the door scraped forward so that the others could only see his outline in the gloom as he peered round it. Any second he might force the door shut. Peter glanced at Charles, the big man's usually ruddy complexion had paled slightly. He sensed himself trembling. Which was ridiculous, these were the ramblings of a senile farmer who, anywhere else, would have been committed to a geriatric hospital. Yet, it was the expression in those eyes, the sheer terror, which rooted them to the step, the power of the Ancient Mariner reborn in a remote valley.

'Aye,' Macgregor's voice was a throaty whisper, 'they screamed for maybe ten seconds and I heard the splashings, the threshings, of whatever it was that got them. Then there was just silence. I came back home and nobody has ever heard o' my father or Ferguson since. The ghillies went to look for 'em the next day, but there was nothing. I've no bin up to the Moss since, but I'll no go agin. Ever!'

The door finally scrapped shut and they heard a bolt being forced into place, the old man shuffling away into his hermit abode. 'Well, that's that!' Charles spoke with a quaver. 'If you go up on the Moss something will get you and you'll never be heard of again.'

'They probably fell into a bog,' Peter tried to speak louder than a whisper but somehow his vocal cords refused to function fully.

'Just as we might without a guide. So we go back to the hotel, get paralytic in the bar, and drive all the way back to London tomorrow!' Charles's tone was scathing, trying to bolster his waning courage. 'What a bloody waste of time and money!' He consulted his watch. 'Believe it or not, even if this landscape has the appearance of dusk, it is just after ten o' clock in the morning. We have a full eleven hours of daylight...well, gloom, before us. Come on, Peter, a crazy old shepherd wouldn't have deterred us in the old days and, damn it, we're not fifty yet. Let's give it a go. We'll go up to the Moss and take care to keep a firm ground. And, you never know, this low cloud might clear. Another couple of hours and we could be sweltering in blistering August sunshine!' He tried to laugh but it was spoiled by an uncontrollable gulp.

It was a steep climb up Mankwill hill. Remus, the Labrador, forged ahead, kept returning and staring quizzically at his human companions, mutely urging them to hurry. There were innumerable sheep tracks through the thick heather, all leading upwards, criss crossing, veering to both left and right. So long as one continued in an upward direction, Charles decided, they were bound to emerge on the Moss above eventually.

He recalled the place from the map which Stewart had sent him, a kind of plateau amidst the mountains. Like the agent had said, albeit jokingly, if those mountains had been removed they would doubtless have looked down upon the waters of Loch Ness on a clear day. The Loch could not have been more than a mile away, as the crow flies. And, as if to taunt his thoughts, a hooded crow cawed from somewhere up ahead.

They came to a patch of slippery scree, rocks draped with lichen and then, without warning, the land levelled.

The mist had thinned temporarily, they could see maybe a hundred yards.

Scrubland, patches of heather dotted with stunted silver birch and rowans, clumps of gorse. Remus came back to them, whined with a renewed eagerness. They had reached their hunting ground at last.

'What a strange place,' Peter unslung his Purdey, opened the breech and slid in a couple of cartridges. 'Who would expect to find a stretch of flat like this up here?'

'There's sure to be blackgame here,' Charles loaded his own gun, his enthusiasm had returned. A bird or two in the bag and to hell with the weather, their feeling of satisfaction would be all the greater because of the difficulties they had surmounted.

'Let's start walking it up slowly, keep in sight of each other. And watch out for the boggy ground.'

'I think Macgregor's story was pure fantasy,' Peter spoke loudly as if he had to convince himself as much as his companion. 'That Ferguson chap and Macgregor's father probably didn't even fall into a bog. They're probably both buried in the local churchyard. All the same we'll watch where we tread.'

Ten minutes later a blackcock clattered out of a clump of birch. Peter's shot was a clear miss, Charles dropped it stone dead with his second barrel, thumped it onto the springy heather where Remus retrieved it seconds later.

'Bravo,' Peter called, ejecting a spent shell.

The mist was threatening to close in again as if to protect the wildlife of this forgotten mountain habitat. Charles licked his lips, you could taste the damned stuff,

13

like stagnant water coating your palette. And his body was chilling beneath his barbour jacket in spite of their recent exertions. Not just the mist and the dank odour, something else... the stillness. Saplings dripped depressingly, even the crow had fallen silent. He shivered again. Thank God for Peter's double shot, the reports blanketed by dense low cloud which crept across the moorland, but nevertheless the shots were a welcome sound.

'Missed the devil!' Peter was temporarily out of sight but he sounded close. 'Should have had the bugger!' Charles looked around, peered into the grey opaqueness. Where had that darned dog got to? Chasing after the unscathed blackcock, probably, and likely to flush more out of sight. He stopped to listen but there was no sound of a dog crashing around in the undergrowth.

'Where's Remus got to?' He called out to Peter. The reply seemed distant, as though it floated back from beyond the next range of mountains.

'Haven't seen him old chap. No sign of him when I fired, which was unusual, to say the least. He's probably put up a hare and chased it from here to...' *To where?* Which, Peter thought, figured. Remus wasn't properly trained, just a dog which hunted and retrieved by instinct. And then he heard the Labrador, a canine cry which embodied pain and terror, reached its peak and then cut off instantly, left only that eerie silence.

'Christ, he must've got in a bog!' Charles started forward, broke into a shambling run. Panicking, premature grief because it was probably too late, the dog had been sucked down into some stinking mire and was already dead. Heedless of his own safety oblivious of his shooting partner. He caught his foot in a tangled root, fell, picked himself up. Blundering on, calling almost hysterically.

Neither of them have been seen or heard since...

Stupid old bugger, they should put him away! The hooded crow was croaking again, a different note this time, a kind of mocking call. We've got your dog, you're next!

A double shot, the two reports almost simultaneous so that they could have been mistaken for a single blast from a shotgun. Sod, Peter, the selfish bastard! Remus is lost, probably dead, and he's still carrying on shooting. *And then Charles heard Peter scream.* Just once. He tried to tell himself that his companion had shouted for the dog, that the call had been warped out of all recognition by these high altitude acoustics.

But however much he tried to lie to himself he knew that it had been a cry of mortal fear.

And now there was only that awful silence left. You could feel it, hear it, the creeping stillness that came with the thickening mountain mist, touching you with its vile dead fingers, stroking you in readiness for...

Charles turned a full circle, slowly, gun held in readiness, safety catch pushed forward, forefinger resting on the trigger. *Ferguson and old Macgregor had a gun, too, hadn't they?* Fired before they screamed. And never been seen again, alive or dead. The waiting was the worst part, knowing that there was something out there in the mist. Something that saw you, watched you. Stalked you. It had got Peter, the dog too. *And now silently and relentlessly, it was moving in for Charles.*

Suddenly, Charles saw it, thought at first that the

head was that of a deer. A rogue Red perhaps, a giant beast that had no fear of man. But the horns were not antlers, and the body that slithered behind it was like that of some outsize black slug, grossly mutated so that it might have been the figment of a fevered nightmare. Yards of it uncoiling out of the foul opaqueness, glistening evilly in the greyness, stinking as it slimed its way towards him.

He fired twice, blasted that grotesque head at point blank range, but the shot charges did not so much as score the reptilian features; did not slow the advance of the serpentine body. A mouth that stretched and elongated to unbelievable proportions as it fanned him with its putrid breath, sunk its jagged incisors into his fleshly throat before his own scream had even begun.

Charles's final thought was not of his own fate, nor that of his human and canine companions. But in his fear-crazed mind he heard again Stewart's voice crackling on the phone.

'If it wasnae for the mountains in the way, ye'd be able to see Loch Ness from the Moss!'

The Ghouls

(from Graveyard Rendezvous 2)

Guy N. Smith

Their trade was in fresh corpses from the graveyard.

Granger opened his eyes, for the hundredth time, and then closed them again. It was useless peering, for there was nothing but total darkness all around him. He had not even brought a torch with him, for there is little to see when one is encased in a coffin which is a foot short in measurement anyway, and one is forced to draw one's knees up and succumb to excruciating pain brought about by cramp. His left hand rested on the small oxygen cylinder at his side, the mask over his face was oppressive, almost frightening. Yet he knew that without it he would die of suffocation within a matter of minutes.

Once again he nearly gave way to the feeling of blind panic, an instinct that urged him to scream, to beat his fists upon the tightly fastened lid above his head, and then to rip his fingers to shreds by clawing at the highly polished wood.

Time meant nothing to him. He was unable to discern minutes from hours. That metal cylinder was his hourglass. When that ran out, then so would his life. He wondered again if he could trust Pieter, the callow youth who had sworn to return at dawn and feverishly dig down through six feet of fresh earth until he could raise the lid off the coffin. That was, unless the others came first. Granger had never been a religious man, but he prayed they would. His groping fingers now located something else by his side; something metal. Subconsciously he traced the outline of this object, from the tip of the short stubby barrel to the heel of the ivory butt. Yes, that .32 revolver certainly did something to boost his morale, he told himself. Again, he checked that it was loaded. When the time came for him to use it there must be no mistakes.

After a while he dozed, a restless slumber in which he dreamed that his oxygen ran out and he was slowly suffocating, screaming in terror the whole while. Then he awoke, his whole body glistening with perspiration beneath the white shroud.

Somewhere there was a scraping sound, the noise made by steel striking stone, and he felt his pulse quicken, his heart pounded even more wildly. He wished he knew what time it was. The noise was getting louder now, and he knew that the diggers were getting nearer. Was it Pieter, or was it them?

A spade scraped the outside of the coffin, and then for the first time he caught the sound of human voices. They were muffled, indecipherable, but Granger knew that his vigil was over. He rested the revolver comfortably in the palm of his hand and thumbed back the safety catch.

Next came a splintering sound which was almost deafening in the confined space. They were not even bothering to unscrew the lid. They were quite content to prise it off in their urgency to get at the body within.

'That's it!' The voice was muffled, uncouth, and he knew that the lid was now partly removed. 'Give us a hand an we'll be away from here in no time at all.'

Granger was glad that the only light outside came from the stars as they wrenched the lid away, splintering it in the process, for he would not need time to adjust his eyes. He could see them both now. Their features were in shadow, but they were large of build, both dressed in overalls, caps and mufflers, as they stood in the open grave, spades and pick-axes in their hands. Their breath came in short, wheezing gasps after the physical exertion which had been necessary in their task. They were pausing now, glad of their brief respite before they began hauling the "corpse" up on the small pulley which they had brought with them.

The range was no more than a yard at the most as Granger pulled the trigger twice in quick succession, firing through the shroud. The reports boomed and reverberated in the grave, but he knew they would be virtually inaudible any distance way above ground. Both men slumped forward simultaneously, dead before they fell, and never knowing what had hit them.

Granger struggled to his feet, pushing aside one of the bodies which was lying across him. It was all he could do to prevent himself from crying out as his circulation began flowing again, and it was fully ten minutes before he was able to haul himself up to the deserted cemetery above him by means of the pulley ropes which the men had brought with them.

As he scrambled out of that deep oblong hole, a voice greeted him from behind a nearby tombstone. 'Mister Granger, Mister Granger, Sir.' There was fear in every syllable. 'Are you alright, sir?'

'Yes, Pieter,' Granger was his cool self once more now that he had the open sky above him. 'I'll be alright, but we've got to work fast. I see the false dawn is already in the sky. Give me a hand.'

From beneath some flowering rhododendron bushes the man and the boy heaved to lift the white shrouded figure which they had hidden there some hours earlier. Laboriously they struggled until they reached the graveside, where they were able to lower it into the open coffin, using the pulley again. This done, Granger climbed down and stood with his feet unceremoniously upon the two dead men.

He could not resist pulling the shroud aside and taking one last look at the features which he had gazed upon in life for the last twenty years. He could not help thinking that even death had not robbed Marilyn of her beauty.

Systematically, he secured the damaged lid of the coffin before clambering up to Pieter again, and helping him to shovel the earth back into the gaping hole. He regretted that the two body snatchers would have to share the same grave as his late wife but, alas, there was no other way if he was to remove all traces of his night's work.

Soon there was no evidence that the grave had been tampered with. The man and the boy leaned on their spades, each busy with his own thoughts, as the daylight became stronger every minute, destroying the black deeds of the night as though they had never been.

'Was there no other way, Mister Granger?' Pieter was the first to break the silence. 'Could we not have hidden in the bushes and surprised them from above?'

Granger shook his head 'No, Pieter,' he said, 'There was no other way.' He pushed some money into the boy's hand and, buttoning up his overcoat, he strode away into the surrounding woodlands where his car was hidden, experiencing a combined sense of grief and the satisfaction of a job well done.

Professor Granger felt at peace with the world at last. Admittedly, his source of fresh corpses at the research centre had now been exterminated but that mattered no longer to him. Nobody would ever miss the human ghouls whose lives he had snuffed out only an hour or so ago. Except, perhaps, his colleagues in the laboratory. They would never know how it all ended, and that was the best way if the whole team of scientists were to continue their work in harmony.

Guy N. Smith

The Lurkers

(from Graveyard Rendezvous 4)

Guy N. Smith

They lurked in the shadows ready to murder.

Carson had been to see me again. Not that I wasn't expecting him because he came into my office most mornings these days. However, this time I'd felt ill at ease after he'd left, and for a long time I sat at my desk smoking one cigarette after another, staring up at the ceiling and wondering just what the hell I was going to do. I could just pack up, leave town, and lose myself someplace. Or could I? There were hundreds of places I could go, but nowhere was big enough to hide me.

This time Carson hadn't threatened me the way he'd done so often in the past. This worried me. He'd been charming, smiled and chatted about trivialities, and assured me that he meant no harm. I asked him if this applied also to the two not-so-tame 'gorillas' who had not let me out of their sight once for the past three months, guys who went around with loaded automatics in there hip-pockets and wouldn't hesitate to use them. Of course, Carson assured me suavely, pausing to remove the ivory-cigarette holder from his mouth so that he could flash me one of those supposedly reassuring leers, they were only concerned for my safety. They were prepared to buy me out, a six-figure sum for the typewritten manuscript which they wanted so badly, the original notes to be included in the deal, of course.

It was a tempting offer, and I would have parted with it but not for two reasons. First, what was going to happen to me once they had it in their possession? The contents were known only to me. Presumably they had already killed Lycett, the man who made the original rough notes in those two exercise books, so with me out of the way nobody else would know about the contents. How could they be sure that I wouldn't sit down and rewrite the lot from memory? For all they knew I might already have taken a carbon copy. No, there was only one way they could be sure of eradicating the contents of that unpublished literary work forever!

Secondly, I had a duty to the public. If I gave Carson the script I would become an accessory to the organisation of blackmail, drug trafficking, murder, and a whole empire of crime.

I only ever saw Lycett, the author, once. He was a reporter on one of the smaller papers at the time, and it was six months earlier when he had called to see me, the month my grandmother died, in fact. He said he'd seen my articles in the press, and wondered if I'd care to undertake the writing of this particular work on his behalf. I said I'd look through the notes, every page of which was filled with barely legible handwriting. It took me a week to decipher it, and I came to the conclusion that it was the basis of a plot for a highly imaginative novel, compiled by a man who stretched one's own credulity to its very limits. However, I hadn't much work on hand at the time, which isn't a good situation for any freelance journalist, so I worked on it night and day.

Then, one day, I chanced upon a name towards the end of the manuscript which seemed to ring a bell somewhere in my memory. Purely out of curiosity I looked it up in my files, and it was then that I received the first shock in this chain of events which was only just the beginning. Feverishly I began to look up the other characters in this wildly improbable work. One by one I found them, prominent citizens, businessmen, landowners. Every one of them existed in real life. The book Lycett had asked me to write was fact, not fiction! And within its pages were exposed a ring of corruption so vast that the villains would fill one of our leading prisons.

Needless to say, I rang Lycett at his apartment at once, but the call went unanswered. I rang again at intervals throughout the day, but still there was no reply. He could have just been out. I began to feel uneasy, and eventually I decided to go and call on him in person.

It was nine o'clock when I stepped out of the elevator onto the lush carpeting of the floor where Lycett had his flat. As I approached the door I halted in my tracks, a feeling of despair creeping over me. I was almost unable to comprehend the wording of the notice pinned to the door - 'VACANT. TO LET'. It was at this moment that I realised that I would never set eyes on

Lycett again.

The next few weeks found me in a state of acute indecision. What was I to do with the completed manuscript now in my possession? Common sense told me to destroy it, but a sense of loyalty to my fellow men urged me to hold on to it, to hide it. Then Carson approached me, the morning of my grandmother's funeral, and as I joined the mourners my face was white and strained. I had already come to a decision. I knew what I had to do, to protect both myself and my folks, in a way it was a kind of compromise, an insurance of life and safety for us.

Within a week my whole life had become one nightmare game of hide-and-seek. Carson now showed his true colours and threatened me with my life unless I handed the manuscript over to him, but I countered this with the ultimatum that if anything happened to me it would come to light, anyway. Whether or not he believed me, I don't know, but he wasn't taking any chances and I was allowed to live. I also let him know that the death of either of my folks would mean an exposure of his corrupt organisation, too. I was buying time for all of us, as fast as I could, but one day it would run out.

The weeks wore on, weeks of fear and foreboding for myself. My office was constantly under surveillance from the street below, and I knew that the cars which were parked overnight on the piece of waste ground opposite the house where I lived with my mother and father contained Carson's hidden watchers. His Lurkers, the killers who remained under cover of darkness and shadows, waiting.

Once I stood at the window of my bedroom with a loaded shotgun in my hands. The moon was full, and I could see the two men in the parked car clearly. They were less than thirty yards away, and I was tempted to discharge both barrels at them. However, I couldn't have explained my actions to the law, so slowly I unloaded the gun and returned it to its resting place beneath the bed.

In spite of everything I tried to lead a normal life. Five days of the week I went into the office, but mostly in the evenings I stayed indoors. I motored over to see my girl in the next town no more than twice a week, even then taking devious routes in order to throw off my pursuers. Once Carson found out about her it might present him with the opportunity he sought to bargain for the missing manuscript. Jeanette was pretty sore about these infrequent visits, but I couldn't tell her the real reason, and somehow I felt it might be for the best if she left me, distressing as it would be at first.

On Sundays I always went to church, something which I have done throughout my life. I noticed that Carson's henchmen had also joined the congregation, occupying a pew at the back. It amused me to think that I had brought his lurkers into a place of worship.

After the services I made a point of tending to the family grave beneath the tall elm trees, in the furthermost corner of the overgrown courtyard. It was practically the only grave which was regularly looked after amidst this jungle of tall weeds, and I prided myself in its appearance. I washed the headstone with detergent in order to remove the bird-droppings, and cleared an area around it which I planted with lobelia and alyssum. Truly it was a colourful island in a sea of drab desolation.

Below this patch of ground lay my grandparents and great-grandparents. My parents, myself, and any children which I might father will all join them in time, united in death as we have been in life.

And so life went on, day after day, week after week, month after month, and still they watched me. Once they broke into my office, but nothing was taken. They did not find what they were looking for. Once they got their hands on that manuscript I was doomed. But someday it will be found. The death of either myself or my parents will bring it to light. Carson's empire will be shattered. The opening of our family tomb will sweep a tidal wave of destruction over them, for there, resting in the coffin of my grandmother, will be found the wreath which I threw in that grey afternoon, only minutes before the discreetly waiting grave-diggers began filling in that gaping hole. The bunch of lilies will have long rotted away, but packed neatly inside the polythene wrappings at the base of the plastic covering which originally were flowers, will be discovered that manuscript which has been sought by Carson for so long. The fate of those men who have commanded public respect for so long lies below ground level in this neglected and peaceful churchyard. Carson and his men lurk in the shadows of my life, and I just wait.

The Executioner

(from Graveyard Rendezvous 6)

Guy N. Smith

Vengeance smouldered within him as he hunted them down to pay the supreme penalty for their war crimes.

Wolskel had spent over a year preparing his file on Bremmer from the moment he first located the whereabouts of the Nazi Beast. He had followed a meticulous process in just the same way that he had plotted the execution of his former three victims. But this was the big one, the culmination of a hunt to which he had devoted the last twenty years of his life. He could not risk any slip-ups with the coup-de-grace in sight.

Vogel, Stalhein and Duvar had been academic by comparison, 'practice runs' for when he found Bremmer. Certainly all three were Nazi war criminals who had deserved to die for their part in the atrocities during the occupation of Poland. But throughout, Lech Wolskel had pursued Bremmer with a smouldering obsession for revenge, for he had proved beyond a doubt that it was the commandant who had been instrumental in betraying 14,000 Polish servicemen to the Russians and instigating the massacre in Katyn Forest in 1940. The Nazis had been blamed for the outrage but recently the USSR had owned up to the slaughter. But the guilt lay with Bremmer.

Any day in the metropolis you would pass a dozen Wolskels, barely give them a second glance. Executives, civil servants, greying hair, bespectacled and carrying briefcases that denoted a respectability in their daily routine of paperwork and meetings. You saw them on the tubes and on the buses, ignored them because they were part of the accepted background to the bustle of city life. Which was how Wolskel had intended it to be from the first day he had commenced work at Whitehall. His position of trust had allowed him access to secret files. Three down and one to go. After that he might apply for early retirement and return to his beloved homeland, satisfied that his life had been well spent, that his father, who had been one of the Katyn victims, had been avenged. He fought to maintain a calmness. Only when it was all over would he allow himself to gloat.

He returned to his large suburban house, smelled again that lingering odour of death as he entered the long hallway. Its sickly sweetness was like nectar and made him heady. A door at the end of the dimly lit corridor led down to the cellar below, his footsteps echoing in the dank bowels of this place of death.

The light from a single bulb showed him the gallows which he had constructed over innumerable weekends, the rough sawn timbers, the trapdoor which operated with precision; the hempen noose greased so that it slid smoothly and tightened. His eyes travelled over to the far corner where a stone slab covered the 'pit', a deep grave that had taken him months to excavate, and alongside it the bag of quicklime that had already destroyed three corpses and was awaiting a fourth.

His half smile turned to a frown, his lips tightening and his forehead creasing. Now that he had discovered Bremmer's hideaway, unmasked his pseudonym, the commandant should have been easier than the others. Bremmer was an old, pathetic, doddering, octogenarian who would offer little resistance.

He made no attempt to conceal his movements, had long ago convinced himself that he had successfully covered his tracks. And now, with legal protection against those who would have brought him to trial for his war crimes, he basked in the safety of his dingy terraced house. Every evening at nine he shuffled down the street to the pub on the corner, drank two double whiskeys, and returned promptly at ten. Wolskel had watched his intended prey every night for the past week, the other's movements synchronised with his own digital watch. Any night would have done, Wolskel's only nagging fear was that death from natural causes might have cheated him at the final hour. He had almost permitted himself a day or two in which to savour the pending execution.

Until today, when he knew that it had to be tonight. And even tonight might be too late!

Whitehall had received information from one of its most trusted Middle East agents that the Hawk was believed to be in London, having slipped through Heathrow security on the previous day. A man whose very name brought cold sweat to surviving war criminals in their havens throughout the world, a fanatic who executed mercilessly, came and went like a sporadic show of winter sunshine. The agent had reported that the Hawk was believed to have located Bremmer, established proof of his identity as well as his whereabouts, and was poised to kill. That information was not known to The Department, only to Wolskel who had tracked down his man. And now the one known as the Hawk might beat him to it, mock him with a shot blasted or knife hacked corpse. There was no time to be lost.

Wolskel sat in his parked Volvo in the sparsely-lit street, watched the pub in his rear-view mirror. The night was misty, there was a hint of drizzle in the air. Visibility was poor. He glanced at his watch. 21.53. In seven minutes Bremmer would come out of that door, follow the pavement on the shadowy side until he reached number 53. Then he would fumble in his overcoat pocket for his door key and let himself in. Just as he had done on the previous seven nights when Wolskel had sat and watched. Tonight would be no different. It must not be.

It was.

22.05 and there was no sign of Bremmer. Wolskel was tense he felt slightly sick, tried to tell himself that perhaps tonight the Nazi had permitted himself a third double whiskey. He hadn't, he wouldn't, because his makeup was as rigid now as it had been half a century ago.

Wolskel searched the shadows on both sides of the street looking for a lurking figure. He laughed mirthlessly to himself. If the Hawk was here, you wouldn't see him. He shivered uncontrollably.

22.12. Maybe there was a perfectly ordinary explanation for Bremmer's non-appearance. Like he had a cold or a fever, or the night was too chilly for him to go out. Or that he was dead, either from natural causes or...

22.20. Lech Wolskel let himself out of the car, looked up and down the street. There was nobody in sight. He began to walk slowly along the uneven littered pavement until he stood outside number 53. His stomach churned, knotted. For the first time in his life he experienced fear, almost turned and fled. Only the thought of a father who he scarcely remembered stopped him from abandoning his mission. If Bremmer still lived, then he must hang, and his corpse must be destroyed in the 'pit'.

The door was unlocked! Wolskel's outstretched fingers touched it and it creaked, opened a couple of inches. A low wattage bulb burned in the passageway and an odour of staleness wafted through the gap, the stench of an old man's den, a combination of an unwashed body and urine. His hand dropped to the pocket of his overcoat, felt the reassuring bulk of the .38 that nestled inside it. An illegal weapon. He laughed again.

Wolskel stepped inside, left the door slightly ajar behind him. He waited whilst his eyesight adjusted to the gloom. He listened, but there was no sound to be heard. Icy fingertips stroked his spine. Yet he sensed that he was not alone.

A door led off from the narrow hallway. His fingers depressed the handle, it was loose and rattled slightly at his touch. The room beyond was in darkness except for a shaft of light that penetrated the frayed curtains, an eerie glow that denoted silhouettes and created deep shadow. The atmosphere was heavy, almost suffocating, the stench so strong now that it rasped his throat.

Wolskel stood there in the open doorway, felt rather than saw the untidy, unclean room, the dead coals in the fireplace, food scraps on a plate on the table. He stiffened when he picked out the armchair, the huddled shape in it facing away from him. A balding head that slumped forward, legs stretched out. The other was either asleep... or dead!

'Bremmer?' Wolskel scarcely recognised his own voice, the way it quavered, the pistol heavy in his shaking hand.

There was no response. He had begun to back away when the figure in the chair stirred, the head lifted and turned, the features hidden in a patch of shadow.

'Who... is... it?' The voice was cracked, the invisible lips slobbering, but there was no hint of fear in the words. Just a question, curiosity because there was an intruder in the house.

'You wouldn't know my name if I told you,' Wolskel's pulses were racing, he fought against sudden euphoria because neither death nor the assassin known as the Hawk had beaten him to his prey. 'But I know you, Commandant Bremmer. Remember Katyn Forest?'

Then there was a pause, an intake of breath that rattled in aged lungs. Then, 'Yes, I remember.'

'Good. Then you will know why I'm here. I've a car waiting outside. I want you to come with me. If you resist, or try to call for help, I will shoot you dead. Understand?'

The other obviously understood because with some

difficulty he struggled up out of his chair, a gaunt silhouette against the lights from the street outside. He groped on the table, located a greasy trilby hat and jammed his head, pulling the brim down over the other's forehead. He would offer no resistance. Wolskel stood back, motioned for the other to shamble outside ahead of him.

The street was still deserted as Lech Wolskel pushed Bremmer into the passenger seat of the Volvo. The engine purred into life and the car slid smoothly away from the curb. Another glance in the mirror just in case they were being followed. They weren't. The Hawk had been beaten at the death.

*   *   *

Within a quarter of an hour Wolskel was pushing the senile Nazi into the door of his own house, locking it behind him. The other seemed resigned to his fate, obeyed every command, offered no resistance as he was pushed towards the cellar steps, gripped the rail as he descended.

When Wolskel had executed Stalhein he had gone through the process of a 'trial' beforehand. In many ways it had detracted from the purpose of his vengeance. Judge and executioner: the denials, the pleas of innocence, had been rejected. Death by hanging was the only outcome. The evidence in itself was damning, he was not looking for a stay of execution.

Falteringly, Bremmer allowed himself to be led on to the platform, the noose draped around his neck and tightened.

'My Father was at Katyn,' Wolskel's whisper echoed in the confined space. 'That is why I am going to hang you.'

The Nazi did not answer, the only sound was that of the phlegm bubbling in his tired lungs. He made no excuses, no denials. Wolskel was glad that he was unable to see the other's features and made no attempt to confront his victim. He had no wish to look upon the one who had ordered his father's shooting. Death itself would be sufficient, the vile corpse destroyed forever by the lime. Then it would be all over.

With an effort he resurrected his anger, recalled the hatred which was beginning to slip away from him, for without it all this would be futile. He might as well have left Bremmer for the Hawk.

'You bastard!' He forced himself to shout. 'Fourteen thousand lives wasted. Widows and orphans left to grieve. I was one of them. I still am. I've cried for my father night after night. Tonight I will cry no more.'

The shape on the gallows seemed to have taken on a new grotesqueness, the frail body had filled, the neck swelling and bulging, the rough hemp abrasing the bloated flesh. The breath hissed like a steaming kettle as the bound wrists struggled against their bonds.

Wolskel stepped back, suddenly afraid. No, it was a trick of the light, his own nerves were mocking him now that he has got his man. *Go and look at the face, see for yourself. Gaze upon the shrunken flesh of an old man who is now harmless!*

I don't want to see!

'I die for the Fuhrer!'

Wolskel recoiled, those fanatical powerful tones

vibrating his brain, the ringing in his ears shrill and hysterical like fourteen thousand souls screaming for vengeance.

Hang him before it's too late!

Wolskel grabbed for the lever, gripped it with sweaty fingers, sensed the evil that emanated from the man on the platform, a force that came at him with terrifying suddenness. He threw his full weight on the iron handle, it seemed to be defying him, pulling against him. Then it yielded, threw him backwards as it released the platform. A clang as the trapdoor fell, followed by a full second of awful silence in which he thought that his victim was not going to drop, that by some impossible means Bremmer was treading air, mocking the law of gravity.

He cried his relief aloud as he felt the jarring thud, the structure swaying slightly as the falling body was jerked to a spinning halt, heard a loud crack that might have been the .38 accidentally detonating in his own pocket. The gallows vibrated, shuddering like a small ship that had hit an unexpected squall and then eased into a calm.

Lech Wolskel crouched there, smelled his own body odours, then prayed to the God which he had almost forgotten that the Nazi beast was dead; that it was finally over. He trembled and closed his eyes. That inexplicable force, whatever it was, seemed to have gone. He listened to the steady rhythmic swinging of the body below like a metronome that was slowly running down. Until at last it stopped.

You'll have to cut him down, throw him into the pit.

He recoiled at the thought, accepting its logic. No way could he leave Bremmer to rot on the rope, filling the house, which already smelled of death, with the stench of decomposing flesh. He heaved, almost vomited, and accepted what he must do. It would only take a minute or two.

Shakily, Wolskel clambered down the rickety steps, made his way round to the front of the gallows. The corpse had twisted round and thankfully come to a standstill facing away from him. He noted with relief that the body was not bloated, that it was pathetically emaciated in the way it had been prior to the execution. His nerves had got the better of him, and was it any wonder after years of hounding this fiend who was responsible for the cold-blooded slaughter of thousands of his own countrymen?

He reached up and began to saw at the noose with his pocketknife, cutting through the strands for the rope would be needed no more. It had done its work.

His fingers touched the neck flesh and he snatched them away, revolted by the icy coldness of the flesh which should still have been warm. He stumbled, fell back, and stared in horror as the body began to swing round, the gallows creaking with the movement. *Turning slowly, coming round to face him.*

A scream escaped Wolskel's lips as he looked upon those cadaverous features for the first time, dead eyes that found his own and held them with a hypnotic, malevolent stare. The thick lips stretched into a leering grin, mucus bubbling from the flared nostrils.

He tried to scream a second time but the sound became trapped in his throat and he felt his senses beginning to slip from him. For just above the floating orbs was a jagged circular wound out of which slimy greyish matter seeped, streaking the congealed blood; powder burns around the edges where the Hawk's point-blank bullet had ripped into the skull.

Guy N. Smith

Cannibal Island

(from Graveyard Rendezvous 9)

Guy N. Smith

Only human meat would satisfy their hunger.

The passage across the Pacific had been very calm. To the crew of the "Seagull" it had been almost like a pleasure cruise. Under the blue skies the trawler seemed to sail itself, and only the smell of oil had reminded them that they had engines. It had become lazy, dreamlike. Day after day, the skipper, Jack Dunn, had been able to steer an even course with only his fingertips on the wheel. Often, he thought that if they had been a sailing ship only, they would surely have been becalmed in these glassy waters.

They had a cargo of grain and other goods to unload at Hawaii, and skipper Dunn, no less than the crew, was looking forward to a good time ashore while they were reloading for the return to San Francisco. They had done the voyage many times. It was no exception to have good weather, but they had never had better.

Skipper Jack Dunn was a young man, in spite of his spiky beard and windblown yellow hair. His skin was bronze, his cheeks ruddy, and he had a merry twinkle in his blue eyes. He enjoyed life, particularly this freedom of the seas, when he could wear a faded open necked shirt and greasy shorts and he could sing if he liked at the top of his voice, above the throb of the engine, and the soft splash of the water, as the bows cut their way through the crystal-clearness.

Then, with the suddenness of Pacific storms, a hurricane swept over them. The crew sprang to life at the breath of hot wind. It was always doubtful how bad these storms could be. The still sea began to lash itself into white crested waves. They drew in the sales, secured the hatches, working feverishly to be ready for whatever might come.

It was worse than expected. Far worse. The waves rose to mountainous heights. First they rose to the crest, and then plunged down, down so far that it seemed impossible for the ship to right itself. Skipper Dunn clung to the wheel. He could only pray, for nothing else could save them. When there was a cry of "Man Overboard" they could do nothing about it, they were hopelessly off their course, and he was finding the ship almost impossible to hold. A mast crashed, and they shuddered with the added blow, but all sounds were drowned by the roar of the sea and the screech of the hurricane.

Pitching in all directions the only hope of the crew of "The Seagull" was in their ability to keep the ship afloat. All through the night the hurricane raged on.

They hardly expected to see another dawn. It broke through the black cloud and sheets of rain, angry over an iron grey-sea whose horizon was hidden behind gigantic walls of water.

Then there was a splintering, shuddering crash. The shock of it brought "The Seagull" to a standstill in a tournament of spray. Slowly she groaned and seemed to bend, and then began to heave over, sideways.

Skipper Dunn was thrown away from the wheel when the crash came. For a few moments he was stunned: he scrambled up the sloping floor of the wheelhouse and pushed open the door. It stuck at first, but he flung his whole weight against it. The water was coming over the bridge like a waterfall. He could see nothing except the ship subsiding into the water. Here and there he caught sight of a dark head bobbing about in the waves. But what hope? They had on their life belts. The whole Pacific was shark infested. Supposing they were lucky enough to avoid sharks, what were the chances of being picked up? They had not seen another ship for days and were hundreds of sea-miles from any land.

But what had it struck? Was it an uncharted rock? As Skipper Dunn slid down the almost vertical deck into the water, he took a last look at the landscape. He saw an unending line of spray, which shot up to meet the rain. He had a view of the raging sea. But, at the same time, he noticed that the sea on the other side of the spray was much calmer.

His heart leapt. If this was a reef, this might be a lagoon, and if that was so, there would be an island near.

There was no sign of any of the rest of the crew. In a few seconds, the ship would keel over, and he knew she was already breaking up. He must get away from the suction of the sinking haul as quickly as possible.

He struck out across the smoother water. He hoped the others had found it too. The storm was passing fast, and there were breaks in the clouds. The wind had gone screaming on its way.

As the scene cleared, he saw waving palms, and a stretch of golden beach. It was an island after all! With his remaining strength, he swam towards it. He did not even stop to think whether it was inhabited or not. It was a relief to feel the sand beneath his feet. He looked back and saw that the ship had completely disappeared. He plunged his way into some undergrowth and lay still.

When Skipper Dunn awoke, the sun was shining, and the whole scene looked peaceful: blue sea, blue sky and green palms. He shook down a coconut and refreshed himself with the milk. Then he heard voices. At first he thought they were native, but as he crept closer the words became intelligible. It was English, and he recognised that they belonged to his mate, "skinny Jenkins" (because he was a bony, wiry, little fellow) and big Jim Larkin, the giant of the crew, notable for his red hair.

'Be quiet, you fools,' Dunn said to them, and they jumped to see his face break through the undergrowth. 'We don't yet know if this island is inhabited or not - and if it is, whether the natives are friendly. They might even be cannibals!'

'Aw,' answered big Jim with a lofty wave of his hand. 'Cannibals only belong to fairy stories. This is an educated world.'

'Education might not have got as far as these parts,' Dunn retorted. 'In any case, we'd better be careful. Are any of the others here?'

They both shook their heads.

'Haven't seen anyone! Those who went first were swept into the sea. Don't think they noticed the lagoon.'

They decided to make the best of their good fortune in being saved, and set to work to make some kind of shelter. They went down to the beach at low tide and searched among the driftwood for anything that had been washed up from the wreck. They were overjoyed to find tins of provisions, and even a watertight box with revolvers and ammunition. They took one a piece and felt happier that they had some means of defence apart from their knives. Happier? - because it was then they had a suspicion that they were being watched. They were aware of dark forms on the foliage. A face would peer down and then was gone!

As it would turn out, they wouldn't have long to worry. During the night they decided watch must be kept, so one stayed awake every two hours. Awake and alert, too. It was hard for any of them to sleep properly. There was a constant rustling and shuffling in the undergrowth, a breathing and whispering. As whoever it was, was so reluctant to show themselves it was likely that they were afraid. But it was hard to tell. The three men were more than thankful for their revolvers, although they had decided not to shoot unless they were quite sure that these people meant harm.

As it happened, they were not given the chance. Suddenly, silently, hordes of dark beings set upon them, dropping from the trees, and being a moonless night, the seamen were powerless against an enemy who blended with the darkness. They yelled, but there was no one to hear them. The sound of their voices only unleashed howls and whoops from the natives.

Jim Larkin was the one on watch, and he had his revolver knocked out of his hand when the first native dropped on him, with no chance to retrieve it. Dunn shouted to Jenkins not to shoot, but to hang on to his revolver if he could. There were too many natives, and even though the action was not friendly, the position might be worsened by any fight on the part of the seamen.

Dunn stored his revolver in his pocket before the natives bound him and advised Jenkins to do the same. They could talk easily among themselves, certain that their captors did not understand a word.

When dawn came they were marched across the island, their hands tied behind their backs, escorted by some fifty of the savages, who were dressed only in skirts of dry grass and carried spears, who did a kind of war- dance in circles around them.

The island seemed to be quite small, as they crossed it to the opposite shore in less than an hour and their progress was not fast. They emerged from the trees onto a hill, which looked down upon a beach similar to the one on the other side of the island, except that it was more open and was crowned by an enormous stone figure, obviously the god of these people, and similar to such effigies which are found on many Pacific Islands. It was carved from a single piece of stone, about 20 feet high; the face was grotesque and the body decorated with strange symbols.

Dunn and his companions noticed that a fire had been newly lit a short distance in front of the figure, and over it was a large tripod with three stakes hanging down.

'Do you think these fellows are going to kill us?' Jenkins asked timidly.

'So it seems,' Dunn replied, though he was thinking hard about any chance of escape, and felt pretty dismal about it. 'And eat us as well!'

'Who said cannibals were only in fairy stories?' wailed Jenkins.

'Never mind that now,' growled big Jim, 'just let me get my hands free, and I'll show a few of them a real knockout blow.' Big Jim had once been a boxer.

'No good if you could,' said Dunn. 'There are too many of them, better keep quiet and see what happens. No use getting panicky, anyway. Show them how to die like good white men.'

A native who was bigger and fatter than the rest, sat on a stone opposite to the god. Presumably he was their chief or king, as he had a circle of flowers on his head. This opinion was soon confirmed. The prisoners were led up to him, and the guards forced them to their knees. Big Jim cursed them under his breath, but Dunn tried to be pleasant. Perhaps, this man could save them. If only they could make him understand.

But no! The chief grinned and it was not a kindly grin. He showed a row of white teeth and was obviously thinking about his dinner. He signed to the guards, and in spite of Dunn's appeals to him that he wanted to talk, they dragged them away, and tied them to the foot of the god. All the while they kept piling more wood onto the fire and then started a festival dance around the prisoners. Although the seamen did not know, this was a day when they worshipped together, and usually sacrificed one of themselves. Today they believed the god had sent these men for that purpose.

Dunn leaned back against the base of the statue. He felt the stone against his hands and against the ropes, made of creepers, which bound him. The stone was rough! Feverishly, he began to rub. It would be easy to free his hands. If only he could get to the revolver in his pocket! At least he would have the satisfaction of shooting a few before they killed him. Big Jim have been right after all. They should have thought. It was useless to hope people like these would be friendly.

On went the dance. Dunn worked hard with his hands. He whispered to the others, and they were rubbing too. Big Jim had his revolver, planned to knock out the nearest guard and seize his spear.

'Do you see anything on the horizon?' asked Jenkins suddenly.

Dunn looked hard.

'Yes, I do! It's a ship! Oh boy! If only they'll look at this island!'

At that moment his rope broke, but he had to wait for the others.

The movement had to be perfectly timed.

'I shall aim for the chief,' said Dunn. 'Chief or no chief, he condemned us to death are you ready?'

In unison the hands went to the revolvers. Dunn levelled at the chief before the natives realised anything was happening. There was a report, and the fat man rolled over. Some natives ran to him. They howled and shivered. Then they pointed to the prisoners who were still standing by the foot of the god.

Dunn and his companions had decided amongst themselves that they had a point of advantage with their backs to the stone as they were watching that ship.

The natives held a conference over the dead chief. Contrary to expectations, they seemed frightened. Then one tall fellow gave a snort, as if trying to rally their spirits. He took a spear, and posing it in mid air, aimed at Dunn.

Dunn was not taking any risks. He fired again before the native could throw. The spear dropped harmlessly to the ground. The cannibal staggered and fell.

That was enough for the rest of the company. A howl went through them. They were mystified and frightened. Death that came like that was unknown to them. They no longer chattered, but turned and fled down the hill and into the undergrowth.

Dunn and Jenkins still stood at the foot of the god, with their revolvers ready for the change of mind. But it did not happen.

'Climb up this figure and wave your shirt,' Dunn commanded Big Jim. 'It is probably the ship who answered our S.O.S before we struck the reef. If so, they are looking for us.'

Big Jim stuck his toes into the carving and went up speedily. Off came his shirt, and he waved and yelled with all his might.

The reward was not long. 'They've seen us!' he shouted down to Dunn and Jenkins. 'They've dropped anchor and are lowering a boat! We're going to be saved!'

Mr. Strange's Christmas Dream

(from Graveyard Rendezvous 14)

Guy N. Smith

With Christmas came a nightmare, a
mysterious stranger, and a premonition
of death.

The leaden grey sky, which held the promise, or threat,
of snow, finally released the first few fluffy flakes,
allowing them to drift earthwards with a casualness
which had first belied the heavy fall which was to follow.
The last minute Christmas shoppers, hustling through
the crowded High Street, laden with gaily wrapped
parcels, looked skywards, and increased their pace.
Another couple of hours, and everywhere would be
deserted. They would be able to draw up their chairs in
front of blazing log fires, or the electrical equivalent, and
Christmas would have really begun.

Alexander Strange was the modern counterpart of Charles Dickens's Scrooge. His bent and wizened, gnome-like figure was a source of amusement to the town's youngsters, particularly, during the festive season. The street urchins would shout after him as he walked from the small insurance office, where he worked, to his house, only a couple of streets away. Tonight was no exception but, over the years, he had become immune to such ignorance and rudeness so that their catcalls fell on deaf ears.

Soon he was home, the dilapidated door of his suburban terraced house shut, and a gas fire lit. Automatically, he began preparing his evening meal, not the frugal repast which one would have expected from the famous character from fiction, but a good wholesome steak and kidney pie with apple tart to follow. He would eat this over the next three or four days, not rationing himself by any means, yet refusing to purchase those extra few luxuries which would have made his usual routine just that little bit different.

Mr. Strange hummed a tune to himself while he waited for his pie to warm through. This was most unusual, he even admitted this fact to himself, yet it was almost caused by a celebration. Almost... but not quite. There would be no point in wasting money unnecessarily he reflected. Furthermore, it had nothing to do with Christmas it was all on account of that dream which he had had a fortnight ago. Dream? He shivered at the very thought of it, nightmare, was more like it! Automatically his mind recalled the events of that terrible Tuesday night. It could only have been a dream, he consoled himself for it was too late now for it come true anyway.

All the same, he had lived in sheer terror for the past couple of weeks, but at long last he could relax. It had probably all stemmed from the extra portion of stilton which he had had before retiring. It had been nothing but the figment of a slumber troubled by indigestion.

Yet, his nocturnal visitor had seemed too real. Ghostly, was the word, for he swore that he was able to see the old Victorian chest of drawers through the apparition! The ghost of Christmas future! The figure was so ordinary in appearance, though, that it might well have been the butcher's assistant from the shop down the road, clad in an ill fitting suit.

'What do you want?' Quaking Alexander Strange, pulled up the sheets until only the top half of his face was visible. 'Who are you?'

'My name does not matter,' the other's voice seemed unreal, like the finale of a crescendo of echoes in a mountain pass. 'I am merely a messenger. I have been sent to speak with you.'

'What for?'

'To tell you that you will be in your grave 'ere Christmas has passed!'

Mr. Strange could not remember whether he had fallen asleep then, or whether he'd fainted. Whichever it was, when he woke the grey light of a winter's morning was streaming through the chinks in the curtains, and of his midnight visitor there was no sign. It *must* have been a dream!

However, the elderly insurance clerk was taking no chances, and up until he returned home from the office on Christmas Eve he had lived a life of even greater monotony than usual. He took a roundabout route to and from the office each day, avoiding the busy main streets as far as possible, just in case a speeding vehicle happened to mount the pavement! He had his sandwiches at his desk, fearful to venture out of doors at lunchtime, and in the evenings he retired to bed early. As the yuletide season approached he became both apprehensive and relieved. Apprehensive, because if anything was going to happen it would have to be fairly soon now, and he was relieved as he survived each succeeding day. Each night he slept with his bedside light on.

He also took care to eat no more stilton cheese!

As Christmas Eve came, he had only one night left! Alexander Strange congratulated himself as he ate heartily of his evening meal. It was too late for him to be buried until after Boxing Day now. It *did* call for a celebration of some sort, he decided, as he finished his last mouthful of apple pie. Something not too lavish, though! Then, an idea struck him. He would attend midnight mass at the church just up the road. It wouldn't be far to go, and he need not put anything more on the collection plate than a pence piece! It would be an outing at any rate. Yes, he would go to church.

It was snowing heavily when Mr. Strange walked down the dimly lit street towards the lighted and gaily decorated church. Blizzarding would be a better word, he mused to himself, for the flakes were becoming larger and faster than ever causing him to pull up the collar of his shabby overcoat in order to protect himself from the whipping, stinging snow.

It was as he walked up the snow-covered path towards the church door, that a sudden feeling of pity, something which he had never experienced before, came over him. There, close to the track was a huge mound of soil and an oblong hole, boarded over for safety, denoted a newly dug grave. Mr. Strange shuddered. That would be for old Mr. Russell, he told himself. They're burying him the day after Boxing Day. He had had a good innings at eighty-seven. Alexander Strange shivered again. It could have been himself that grave had been dug for. He almost knew what it felt like to be dead!

The service followed much the same pattern as most midnight communions. In spite of the weather almost every pew was full, and he had to be content with a chair and a cushion beside the verger's seat. The congregation were in a joyous mood, the Christmas spirit being evident in their lusty singing of "O, come all ye faithful". Even Mr. Strange felt his melancholy thawing a little.

The vicar, a robust man with a ruddy face and a bald head, gave the final address. He almost faltered in the blessing as his eyes came to rest on the hunched, praying figure of the miser. Yet another sheep had returned to the fold!

The blizzard was heavy as the congregation filed out into the night, receiving hearty handshakes from the jolly clergyman at the doorway. Mr. Strange was one of the first to leave, being nearest to the exit.

'How nice to see you, Mr. Strange!' The vicar pumped the other's bony, gnarled hand, heartily. 'I do hope we shall see you again soon. Sunday, perhaps…? Ah, Mrs. Watson, how is your dear mother progressing?'

Alexander Strange stepped out into the driving snow. Somehow, he felt more at peace with the world, calmer perhaps. Yes, it would be a good idea to attend matins on Sunday. A very good idea. He might even put two pence in the offertory plate this time!

Suddenly, he felt his feet slipping in the snow. He attempted to regain his balance, but the slippery surface offered no chance of a secure foothold. His legs shot from beneath him, and there was an ear splitting crack of bone on tarmac as his head met with the pathway. Somebody screamed as the huddled, lifeless figure of the old miser gathered momentum on the steep incline. Faster and faster it slid, until it finally hit the concrete kerbstone and shot into the air. It seemed to hang, suspended in space, and then there was a terrific splinter of wood, a rumbling of soil and stone, finally terminating in a shocked silence among the horrified onlookers.

The plump vicar was the first on the scene, producing a small pocket torch from the beneath his flowing robes, and shining the beam down through the splintered planks into the yawning grave beneath. In a yellow circle of light he saw the huddled form of Alexander Strange lying there, his head twisted at a grotesque angle, half buried beneath the pile of excavated soil which his falling body had brought down with it.

Perhaps it was an illusion, a figment of an imagination fired by the horrific scene which lay below him, but the vicar fancied that he saw a figure standing on the opposite side of the grave, a very ordinary man dressed in an ill fitting suit who smiled and nodded his head in a satisfied manner. However, when the clergyman shone his torch in that direction again there was nothing to be seen except softly falling snowflakes, and an impenetrable blackness beyond.

Guy N. Smith

The Case of the Ostrich Slasher

(from Graveyard Rendezvous 16)

Guy N. Smith

A Raymond Odell detective story.

In the 1960s Guy created a fictional detective and wrote a few short stories about him. Raymond Odell, the aquiline featured private eye and his young assistant, Tommy Bourne, work akin to several 'tec duos of the 'pulp' era. Sadly these private eye stories no longer exist today except for collectors who search car boot sales, second hand bookshops and book fairs. Detective fiction today is much more sophisticated, based on police procedure and modern technology. DNA has killed off the good old-fashioned detective stories where the hero had to rely upon his wits and powers of observation and was often called in to assist an official colleague. So Guy has written an original Odell yarn in the old style especially for those nostalgic readers and to introduce to our younger fans a good old-fashioned mystery tale. Study the clues as you go and see if you can beat Odell to the solution.

'The police will get some bad press if we don't get to the bottom of this one in double quick time, Odell,' Detective Chief Inspector Richmond's expression was one of concern. 'Animal lovers will raise a big stink over a mutilated ostrich than ever they would over a murder. And with this "Phantom Horse slasher", as the press have dubbed him, still at large the public will accuse us of dragging our heels because we are not concerned about animals. Clearly this is the work of a maniac even if it isn't the guy who has already carved up half a dozen horses and ponies.'

'Perhaps.' Raymond Odell was on his hands and knees beside the dead ostrich which resembled a heap of bloodied feathers. His fingers eased back the feathers and revealed several gaping wounds where a sharp blade had delved deep and gouged. 'I would've thought an ostrich would have been a darned sight more difficult to catch and mutilate than an equine, one kick from these birds can kill a man stone dead, and a peck from this beak could... hmmm, that's interesting.' His long slender fingers probed the neck, revealed an abrasion of the skin beneath.

'What is it, Chief?' Tommy Bourne peered over Odell's shoulder.

'Almost as if whoever did this throttled it first,' Odell reached his powerful lens out his pocket, examined the mark intently. Then he held up a strand of what appeared to be coarse hair.

'Any ideas, Odell?' Richmond was anxious; impatient.

'Maybe, maybe not.' Raymond Odell straightened up, smiled. The other two knew well enough that if the detective had found a clue then he would not reveal it until his deductions were complete. 'I think we'll go and have a chat with the Masons first and see where we go from there.'

'A few years ago ostrich farming was something that was going to make anybody brave enough to change from conventional farming filthy rich,' Don Mason was in his early forties but his features were etched with lines caused by worry. 'Then, as you've probably read in the papers, everything began to fall apart. We're struggling to survive, and the loss of this stud bird will virtually knock us for six. If we could have reared some healthy stock from him then we might've made it. He cost us two grand, now look what some maniac's done to him...and us!'

'Where does one buy birds like ostriches from?' Odell asked as if it was a matter of casual interest.

'A company calling itself Ostrich International Ltd,' Jane, Mason's petite blonde wife, answered. 'A fly-by-night enterprise. They must have taken hundreds of thousands of pounds from folks like ourselves.'

'Do you employ any farm workers?'

'Only at very busy times,' Mason replied. 'Casual labour, if and when we can get it. We were lucky last week, there's a circus comes to town once a year and they camp on a stretch of common about a mile from here. One of the performers needed some extra cash for a few days in between acts. He was a good worker, a guy named Porson. Kept himself to himself, I'd rather it was like that. Don't even know what he did at the circus, I never asked and he didn't volunteer any information. He stopped on for a couple of days after the circus moved on, then left to join them. Don't expect we'll see him again. I can't afford him now,' he added wryly.

'Where's the circus moved to now?' Odell's eyes narrowed.

'They always go from here to Radwick, about twenty miles away. I presume they've followed their regular itinerary this year.'

'Interesting,' Odell said once they were back in the car. 'How do you two fancy a visit to the circus? We better have a word with this Porson fellow but first I think we'll watch a performance incognito. I haven't been since I was a boy.' He laughed softly to himself as Richmond and Tommy exchanged glances.

Jeffrey's Circus was clearly a low budget show as Richmond remarked to Odell as they sat in the sparse audience. The two clowns had been clumsy and unfunny, the trapeze artist's "stunts" were little more than gymnastics. 'And that lion,' Richmond grunted, 'is old and toothless.'

'And sedated,' Odell grimaced.

The lion ambled out of the ring behind Marcus, the trainer. There was a lengthy pause and then Joseph Jeffrey, clad in worn and frayed ringmaster's attire, announced that, 'You are now about to witness, ladies and gentlemen, the cowboy right from the wild west. Allow me to introduce you to Buckaroo Bill!'

Tommy's boredom soon vanished. The cowboy, in authentic clothing, sat on his horse with ease and skill, whirled a lariat with true expertise. Then, from the entrance tunnel, bounded a half-grown calf. Buckaroo Bill whirled his lasso, threw it deftly over the animal's head, rolled it kicking and twisting in a cloud of sawdust. In one perfectly coordinated movement he leapt from his mount, trussed the calf with a length of rope. Then he turned to the audience, swept his Stetson from his head and bowed to the applause.

'I think we'll have a word with Mister Jaffrey after the show,' Odell muttered to Richmond.

'Can't see how all this figures in the business of the mutilated ostrich,' Richmond answered and then fell silent. Whatever his unofficial colleague suspected, he was unlikely to explain until his suspicions were either proved or disproved.

'We're finishing at the end of the summer,' Joseph Jeffrey was clearly ill-at-ease with the presence of the detectives. His caravan was shabby and basic, proof enough that circuses were no longer money-spinning enterprises. 'Kids today don't want circuses, they'd sooner watch videos or play computer games. If we get out this year we'll just about break-even. I was a fool to think that we could make a success of a continental tour. Holland was a disaster, hardly anybody turned up for the shows and we had to hire animals. Marcus refused to perform with a lion he didn't know and we forked out a grand for a blooming ostrich for Buckaroo Bill to lasso. That was the best part of the show.'

'An ostrich?' Odell snapped, 'But you haven't got it now?'

'No,' Jaffrey gave a wry smile. 'Had to go into quarantine. Six bloomin' months without our best act, couldn't afford to wait. So I sold it to a firm I read about in the papers which sells ostriches to farmers. At least I recouped some of my losses that way. They collected it from the quarantine place themselves.'

'I see,' the detective mused. 'Can you remember the name of the firm you sold it to?'

'Some silly name,' Jeffrey tilted his top hat, scratched his thinking grey hair. 'Somethin' like ... yes, I remember now, Ostrich International.'

'Incidentally,' Raymomd Odell's eyes narrowed, 'that lion in the ring tonight. It was sedated.'

'Sure,' Jeffrey dropped his gaze. 'Begbie sees to that, he used to be a vet.'

'Used to be? I thought it was "once a vet, always a vet" even if you weren't actually practicing.'

'He was struck off, some illegal operations he carried out. Served time for it. But he's useful here, keeps the old animals going and mucks in generally.'

'Hmmm.' Odell mused. 'That cowboy, Buckaroo Bill, he seems to know his stuff, alright.'

'He's genuine. Not a cowboy, of course, but he used to be a horse trainer. Begbie found him for us and he's proved to be the best act in the circus. Bill Porson is his real name. If only we could have got the ostrich back here, things might have been different. Mind you,' he added ',over in Amsterdam, we had to give the ostrich a shot of something to quieten it down, otherwise it would have kicked both Bill and his horse out of the ring, maybe gone berserk on the audience, too.'

'Thank you, Mr Jeffrey,' Odell smiled, 'you have been most helpful. Now, my colleagues and I will leave you in peace for an hour or two, although we may have need to return. Might I request that you keep our visit confidential?'

'Oh, sure,' the circus owner looked relieved. 'Last thing I want is for my lot to know the cops have been around making enquiries. You know,' he winked, 'in this game you take on any casuals who come your way and some of them might've done things which are no concern of mine. But so long as they do the work who am I to question their private lives?'

As they walked back across the tract of waste ground upon which the circus was situated, Raymond Odell suddenly stopped and turned. The others watched as he went over to where the horse which Porson had ridden in his act was tethered. Beside it, draped over the fence, was the lasso. Odell lifted up the length of frayed rope, examined it carefully before plucking a strand from it. He placed it carefully in his wallet and Tommy recognised only too well that hint of a smile on his chief's face.

'Any clues?' Richmond voiced his and Tommy's curiosity upon their return to the local police station although he knew only too well that he was wasting his breath.

'We're slowly making progress,' Odell replied non-committal. 'Now, if I may have the use of the station telephone for ten minutes or so I think we might progress even further.'

It was a quarter of an hour before Raymond Odell emerged from the police inspector's private office.

'Richmond,' he addressed his Scotland Yard colleague, 'did you notice, some months ago, an account in the papers about a rather daring robbery in Amsterdam?'

'You mean the theft of the Tiggelovend tiara?' Richmond grunted. 'Interpol circulated us with the details. It was on show at the jewellers and the shop was ram-raided. The thief escaped with the tiara but there was no way such an item would be able to be offered for sale, it is too well known.'

'That's the one.' Raymomd Odell smiled. 'It has never been recovered to this day and the Dutch police don't anticipate ever finding it. Right now it's probably sitting in some crooks private collection.'

'How does that figure in our enquiries?'

'Because that ostrich came from Holland,' Odell replied. 'And then it died in quarantine, I am informed.'

'The customs officers would have noticed if the bird had been wearing the tiara! Anyway, the ostrich is dead.'

'Exactly,' Odell answered. 'The ostrich died but a similar stud bird was purchased from Ostrich International Limited by the Masons.'

Richmond shook his head this was all becoming too involved and unlikely for him, but he knew Odell of old. The private detective had somehow made a connection between the bird that had died and the one that had been savagely mutilated.

'We're going back to Jeffrey's Circus,' Raymond Odell announced. 'The inspector has kindly agreed to co-operate and has delegated a couple of CID officers to accompany us. Unless I miss my guess we are dealing with desperate men.'

This time Raymond Odell did not head directly for Jeffrey's caravan. Instead, followed by Tommy and Richmond with the CID officers bringing up the rear, he walked towards a small crudely constructed corral in which the man who dubbed himself Buckaroo Bill had just lassoed and thrown a lively calf. A second man was kneeling over the trussed animal, a hypodermic syringe in his hand. Both whirled around guiltily at the sound of footfalls.

'What's going on?' The man attempted to conceal the syringe behind his back.

'I might ask you the same question,' Odell pushed open a makeshift gate and stepped inside the enclosure. 'I take it you must be John Begbie?'

'That's me,' the other scowled. 'So what?'

'Just that at the very least my official colleagues here may arrest you for being in possession of and administering controlled substances. I see that not only do you sedate the poor old lion but you also slow down a lively calf.'

'It's in the interest of public safety,' Begbie backed away a step.

'Perhaps.' Out of the corner of his eye Odell noticed that the other four were now inside the corral. 'I believe both of you went on tour in Holland with the circus last July?'

'That's right,' Porson looks less convincing without his western clothing. 'It wasn't a success.'

'Neither for Mister Jeffrey nor for yourselves,' Raymond Odell's searching gaze flicked from one to the other. 'In fact, many thousand pounds worth of stolen property has gone missing and, it seems, will never come to light again. I refer, of course, to the famous Tiggelovend tiara.'

'Never heard of it,' Begbie growled, took a step

backwards.

'Most certainly you have,' Odell saw the two CID men, with Richmond and Tommy, closing in on the vet and the self-styled cowboy. 'In fact, you ram-raided it from an Amsterdam jewellers.'

'That's rubbish,' Porson's laugh was forced.

'No,' Raymond Odell continued, 'you stole the tiara and that's when your problems began. You knew there was no chance of selling such a famous item intact so your prised the valuable diamonds out of it, and the crown itself is probably now residing at the bottom of a fjord. Your other problem was how to smuggle the stones back to England so you hit upon an ingenious plan. Using your veterinary skills, Begbie, you implanted the diamonds in the body of the ostrich which Jeffrey had purchased while on tour. You knew full well that the bird would have to be kept in quarantine upon your return to England but you were prepared to stick with the circus and bide your time until the ostrich was returned to Jeffrey.'

'What a load of rubbish!' Porson laughed again.

'Unfortunately for yourselves,' Odell went on, 'Jeffrey was desperately short of money. So he sold the ostrich straight from quarantine to Ostrich International Ltd who supply breeding stock to ostrich farmers. Unfortunately, the poor bird which carried a fortune around with it died. The Masons, whom you know, purchased an almost identical bird. You contacted Ostrich International, on the pretext of wanting to purchase a fine male bird for stud purposes, and discovered that such a bird had been sold to the Masons. Naturally the firm did not tell you that the bird from quarantine had died. So you had to get the diamonds out of the Mason's bird.'

Porson and Begbie glanced around them uneasily; the three policemen and Tommy had moved in on them.

'Porson, you took a casual job at the Masons' farm to suss out the situation, and you were convinced that the stud ostrich there was the same one that you and Begbie had put the diamonds inside. By this time the feathers would have grown again over the incisions where the diamonds were implanted and you wouldn't know for certain if it was the one until you started cutting it open. Catching an ostrich is far from easy.' Raymond Odell smiled. 'So the other evening you went to the Masons' farm after dark and Buckaroo Bill performed this act for real and lassoed the ostrich. For your information, a strand from the frayed lariat,' Odell pointed to the rope that dangled from Porson's grasp, 'adhered to the feathers and I have since matched it with the rope it came from, the one you are now holding. I was also puzzled by the wounds in the ostrich; a maniac would have slashed and stabbed, but these were deep gouges and probes. I concluded that the attacker was hacking for something specific beneath the skin rather than simply inflicting a series of cruel wounds. My conversations with Ostrich International and Interpol completed my jigsaw and now ...'

Begbie and Porson sprang into action, would have dashed for the fence and tried to escape, but the detectives were too quick for them. Tommy's rugby tackle brought down Porson, whilst the CID officers leaped upon Begbie and bore him to the ground.

From the doorway of his battered caravan, Jeffrey

watched and shook his head sadly. His touring circus would not even last until the end of the year now.

'Well, I never thought a senseless act like the slashing of an ostrich would lead to the solving of an international crime,' Richmond shook his head in disbelief.

'Which just goes to show,' Raymond Odell laughed, 'that you never know what the outcome will be when you embark upon the most seemingly trivial of investigations. I treat them all the same initially, no detail must be overlooked, no matter how irrelevant it might seem. As they say, you never know...'

The Werewolf Legend

(from Graveyard Rendezvous 19)

Guy N. Smith

Do werewolves really exist?
The legend goes back thousands of
years and, as the saying goes, there is
no smoke without fire.

The werewolf is the ultimate in evil and depravity, a
legendary creature which dates back to time immemorial
although the word 'werewolf' is Anglo-Saxon. Many
countries throughout the world have their 'were'
creatures. India has its were-tigers, Africa its were-lions
and were-crocodiles although the origins of the legends
are lost in the mists of time.

First, though, just what is a werewolf? It is a creature
which is half-man, half-wolf, the strength and cunning
of the animal taking over from the logic of the human
being during the period of the full moon. A person may
live an otherwise normal life, but during that terrible

week of each month it reverts to the sub-human, the bloodlust uppermost in its crazed brain as it lavishes its victims mercilessly.

As the full moon rises the change from man to beast begins. The skin becomes coarse and hair begins to grow over the entire body. The features become enlarged and distorted, powerful fangs and razor-sharp claws enable him to savage man and beast, eyes glinting redly as he stumbles across the countryside, lurking in the shadows and baying the moon frequently.

The moon is the key to the existence of this terrible creature. Without it he is powerless, once it begins to wane and dawn breaks he must return to human form, slinking home, tortured by guilt and remorse at his nocturnal ravages. He is fully aware of everything that has happened, and powerless to prevent it happening again the following night.

The werewolf, though, can be identified even when in human shape. Those afflicted with the curse are reputed to have the third finger of each hand longer than the others, and during the Middle Ages, particularly in France and Germany, people were burnt at the stake purely on the evidence of this malformation. The creature is closely allied to the vampire, but there is one main difference, namely the latter is dead whilst the former is very much alive. After death, though, unless killed in the prescribed way, which is dealt with later in this article, the werewolf becomes a vampire. The curse is eternal. The soul knows no peace.

The legend was at its height during the Middle Ages, and there were two main ways in which one became one of the creatures of the damned. Auto suggestion, known as lycanthropy, was undoubtedly the most common, and here myth becomes reality. A person *believed* himself to be a werewolf whilst in fact no actual physical change took place during the phases between the full moon. It was a form of madness which today results in one becoming a psychopath.

The other method is when one is bitten by a werewolf. It this way the curse can spread like an outbreak of plague, and many of the very early stories concern remote villages where a large percentage of the inhabitants were werewolves.

In both cases the sadistic side of the sexual instinct is the dominant force. Some legends refer to a person making a pact with the devil, and in return receiving abnormal strength. One who has traded his soul for power is granted his wish in the most terrible way possible.

Yet there is a link between legend and reality. Whilst we have established that today the werewolf had been replaced by the psychopath the old beliefs still linger. Before the outbreak of war Adolf Hitler formed his 'Werewolf Organisation'. This consisted of a band of ruthless killers who inflicted terrible atrocities upon their enemies, people who openly opposed the Nazi movement. These men killed by night and, in a country whence the werewolf legend originated, created an aura of terror.

There is another school of thought which believes that the werewolf is an astral projection, yet if this were so the beast would not be able to inflict terrible wounds on its victims.

Whist there is no evidence to suggest there having

been werewolves at any time during history, we must bear in mind the superstitions which were rife during the Middle Ages. There were many who sought to use the Forces of Darkness for their own ends, and we must not underestimate the powers which are beyond our comprehension.

Whilst many barred their doors and windows during the time of the full moon, there were others who sought to destroy the creatures which spread terror and destruction. The most common method of all was to shoot the accursed with a silver bullet. Silver is greatly feared by vampires, and many people wore silver crosses to keep them safe from the undead.

It is also a well known belief that a werewolf cannot cross running water. Again this is something which applies to a vampire, and should either of these mythical creatures chance to fall into a stream or river then their end is assured. A person known to be a werewolf, who dies from natural causes whilst in human form must have a wooden stake driven through his heart to prevent him from becoming a vampire after death.

Let us now look in closer detail at the man who is under the curse of the werewolf. This follows a pattern throughout history, and although situations change, the basic principles still apply.

The farmworker has been bitten by his sheepdog. Little does he realise that this dog has in turn been bitten by a werewolf which has been savaging the sheep in the surrounding area for the past few months. The disease is carried in the saliva, and when the next full moon rises, the man undergoes a terrible experience. He is awakened in his bed by a burning sensation throughout his body, yet it is not unpleasant. It is as though power is being pumped into him, evaporating his human frailty. He rises from his bed, irresistibly drawn towards the window where he stares up at the silver orb in the night sky. It has a kind of hypnotic effect on him, but even this cannot nullify the shock which is his when he notices the state of his body. His arms are longer, falling below his knees, and his instinct is to walk on all fours. But this is not all. His skin is covered with coarse, matted hair and his calloused fingers have turned into claws with sharp ragged nails. His night attire falls from him in shreds, the seams bursting under the strain of an enlarged torso. He recoils in horror as he catches sight of his reflection in the mirror. His head is that of a wolf, huge yellowed fangs, wide nostrils, small eyes that glow redly.

But his terror is only short-lived. It is replaced by a sense of elation. He is the supreme being, stronger and faster than any living creature and far more cunning. He glances at his wife sleeping in the bed which he has just vacated, yet he does not feel any bestial urge towards her, and dropping on to all fours he pads softly from the room without waking her.

It is amazing how, throughout hundreds of werewolf stories spanning four or five centuries, a wife is seldom woken by her husband's 'change' and neither does she have any suspicions concerning his curse.

Once outside he pauses to bay the moon, a fearful howl which chills the blood of the villagers cowering in their beds. They have heard werewolves before, or else the stories told to them by their forefathers are so vivid that they have no trouble in recognising the killing cry.

Force of habit has ensured that their doors are barred when the moon is full, and now they will pass a sleepless night until daybreak.

The werewolf, meanwhile, is crazed by the thought of fresh blood and raw meat. He must savage and eat at the earliest opportunity. In the distance he hears the bleating of sheep, and breaks into a fast lope. Even on this first occasion he shows remarkable cunning, using the wind to his advantage and keeping to the shadows so that he surprises an unwary flock of sheep, and as they break into a panic-stricken run he overhauls them with unbelievable speed and fells one with a blow from a mighty paw.

The feeding habits of the werewolf are the most disgusting of all legendary creatures. The vampire is delicate and seductive, leaving only a small mark where he pierces the jugular vein and drinks the blood of his victim, the 'kiss' with which we are all familiar in stereotyped films of this kind. However, the man-wolf knows no such niceties. His sharp claws rip his prey to shreds in a matter of seconds and greedily he begins to cram the bloody flesh into his cavernous jaws, munching and slurping his delight. But the worst is yet to come, as he disembowels the unfortunate sheep, its intestines a delicacy which he savours once his initial appetite has been appeased. Only the fur is left as evidence for the terrified shepherd to find after daylight. He howls his thanksgiving to the moon again, a long drawn out cry which those cringing in their beds in the village below recognise as the 'killing cry'.

The werewolf moves on. Not until the sky begins to lighten in the east will he return to his bed. Now he will kill for the sake of killing, possibly drinking more blood but leaving the flesh. He may pursue the rest of the frightened flock of sheep, dropping them one by one until the field is strewn with his carnage, or he may travel further afield hoping to surprise an unwary shepherd who has stopped out with his flock.

The moon is waning fast as the werewolf, his fur matted with the congealed blood of his victims, returns to his home. His wife still sleeps soundly; she is the only villager who has not heard the howls of the killer! The change back to human form is rapid, the deformations reverting to normal within a few minutes. Now his terror begins as he remembers his atrocities, but he crawls back into bed and hopes that it will not happen again. He hides the remains of his tattered night attire, perhaps taking them out into the fields with him and burying them, and prays that nobody will discover his secrets.

But the curse grows stronger. The following night with the rising of the full moon he is abroad again. This time, he happens on a luckless girl from the village, wandering home after visiting her boyfriend, and ravages her.

So it goes on. The villagers know that one of them is a werewolf, but they are too frightened to venture out after darkness. Except the blacksmith who fashions himself a silver bullet for his gun. He knows that he can kill the beast with it but his task will be a lengthy and dangerous one for he, too, must be abroad beneath the full moon, hoping to come up on his quarry, praying that he will not fall into the clutches of those jaws and feel the hot fetid breath on his face.

At last, after months of perseverance, he stalks the

werewolf as it feeds on a freshly killed sheep. His bullet is true, but the creature does not roll over. Instead, with a cry of anguish, it lopes away leaving a trail of blood in its wake on the hoarfrost. Next morning the farm worker is discovered in his bed, a jagged bullet wound in his body. The villagers rejoice at the lifting of the curse, but only the blacksmith is worried. Is this the end of it all or has the farm worker passed on the werewolf curse to one of his victims and when the next moon rises the terror will start all over again?

This is the theme of almost all of the werewolf stories of centuries past. Situations vary, perhaps the killer falls into a gushing stream, but basically the legend follows a pattern.

From the point of view of today's addict to werewolf stories the old theme is hackneyed and boring, yet the 'pulp' magazines of the twenties and thirties were able to hack it up in generous servings simply because it was the original legend told in its country of origin. However today the werewolf is still as popular as ever, but his depredations are spread further afield. We read of his exploits in the towns and cities and he's found in countries other than those on the continent.

And why, indeed, should Britain not have its own werewolf stories? Once wolves roamed our forests and if we are to indulge in the fantasies of the Germans and the French, then surely our own fields and forests were plagued by creatures which were half-man, half-wolf.

Horrors have come and gone over the years. We read of plagues of outsize creatures whose ravages make those of the werewolf seem trivial by comparison. Yet the werewolf legend has lasted for centuries. The answer to this lies within ourselves. Even in the midst of civilization our subconscious fears the darkness and the unknown. Did something move in the shadows between the street-lamps or was it our imagination? The fields and woods are at their most beautiful by moonlight yet we cannot dispel that slight shudder or the quickening of a heartbeat. If such creatures as werewolves existed in days gone by are they extinct or, like the legend, have they lived on, the curse being handed down from father to son?

Logically, we tell ourselves, they are a figment of the darker side of the imagination of mankind but deep within ourselves we still fear them. The howling of a dog on moonlit nights or the soft padding footsteps of a prowling fox are magnified a thousand times, and we are grateful that our doors and windows are barred, and that we are safe within the confines of a modern house on a conventional estate.

The werewolf knows no boundaries and the legend will go on forever more.

Guy N. Smith

The Howling on the Moors

(from Graveyard Rendezvous 35)

Guy N. Smith

'There it goes again!' exclaimed a bewildered Tommy Bourne, turning to look at his chief in the bright moonlight. 'Do you think there really is a wolf at large?'

'We'll know soon enough, Tommy,' replied Raymond Odell, the Brook Street detective, 'it's getting closer all the time.'

The two detectives were crouched behind a low stone wall. The moonlight shone all around, casting shadows and creating an atmosphere of unreality. This was a very lonely part of the Sussex coast and from where they were they could just make out the sea about a quarter of a mile away, where the moors dipped down to join the stony beach.

The moonlight glinted eerily on the waves. They were reminded once more of their reason for being in such a place in the dead of night. There had been reports of a large ghostly wolf, which had put in several appearances over the past few weeks on this part of the coast, and eventually these stories had reached Scotland Yard. As far as the police could see no crime had been committed, and they were far too busy with much more important matters to bother investigating what was probably mere local gossip. However, the reports continued to come in, and finally Detective Inspector Richmond had asked Raymond Odell to combine work with pleasure, take a holiday in the area concerned and see what it was all about.

Suddenly Odell gripped Tommy Bourne's arm with steel-like fingers. 'Look!' he whispered, 'there it is, Tommy, amongst those rocks on the top of that hillock!'

The two detectives wasted no time, and keeping as low as possible, using every scrap of available cover, they began to weave their way towards the ghostly apparition. Raymond Odell was comforted by the fact that he had his service revolver in the pocket of his overcoat. He was taking no chances until he knew what this was all about.

Suddenly Odell went sprawling as he stumbled over something in the long grass at the bottom of a slight incline and Tommy, following close behind, fell on top of his chief. They picked themselves up, and the beam from Tommy's pencil torch disclosed the object they had fallen over. It was the body of a man, and from the way he was lying, in a twisted grotesque heap, there could be no doubt that he was dead. Odell's aquiline features had a grim look about them as he viewed the man's face in the light of the torch.

'It's Marty Wiseman,' he snapped, 'he's only been out of prison a few months. You remember him, don't you, Tommy? He's the chap they couldn't pin that coast guard's murder on some time back, and he only went down on a charge of smuggling.'

Before the young detective could reply, the night air was shattered again by that terrible howl. Reminded of their initial task once more, the two men plunged after the ghostly form which was still visible amongst the rocks above them. Odell now had his revolver in his hand. One moment the beast was visible, the next it had completely vanished.

When Raymond Odell and Tommy Bourne reached the place where they had seen it there was nothing but rocks and stony ground. They searched the area in the hope of finding a clue to the mystery, but there was no clue to be found, not even a footprint.

'We'd better get back and have a look at Wiseman's body,' Raymond motioned to his companion.

A further shock awaited them, for the body had disappeared! Completely disappeared. Raymond Odell was not a man to stand still with amazement. Seconds later he was on his hands and knees, followed by Tommy Bourne, carrying out a minute inspection of the ground around where the body had lain.

Suddenly a satisfied exclamation burst from his lips. 'See these footprints,' he snapped, directing the beam of the torch onto the grassy surface, 'Wiseman wasn't dead, only shamming. That wolf was a decoy. While we were chasing it, Wiseman got away. We must have surprised him earlier on, and his only chance was to sham death and rely on the wolf. And these footprints,' he shone his torch on another set a few feet away, 'were made by somebody who joined him, probably the man who set up the decoy. See that sawdust in the footmarks? That can mean only mean one thing. There isn't a woodyard in these parts, so they can only have come from the sawdust covered floor of the 'Old Mariner,' that pub that stands on its own about a mile down the road.' There was a grim look on the detective's face. 'Late as it is, Tommy, we're going to pay the landlord of the 'Old Mariner a visit!'

No lights were showing at the inn when Raymond Odell brought his car to a halt outside. He and Tommy got out. They pounded on the door for a full five minutes before a light finally came on, and they heard footsteps shuffling down the stairs. There followed the sound of heavy bolts being drawn back, and a red bearded giant of a man appeared in the lighted doorway. Before he could speak, Odell thrust a printed business card into the man's hand followed by a curt, 'We'd like to have a word with you.'

Roker, the landlord, seemed taken aback, perhaps frightened, and he motioned for them to step into the sawdust strewn, untidy bar. He waited for Odell to speak, but before the detective could fire a staccato question at the other, a dismal howl came from below their feet. Roker cowered back.

'So that's where you keep your wolf, is it?' Raymond Odell rapped. 'Chained up in the cellar.'

Another howl rent the night air, but this time from outside. Tommy Bourne was at the window in two strides pulling back the shutters. There was nothing in sight. Next second a shot rang out. Odell and Tommy dropped to the floor, seeking cover but the bearded landlord slowly sank to his knees, a crimson stain spreading across his chest.

For some minutes the detectives kept low, and then Raymond Odell wormed his way across the room. Reaching up, he pushed the shutters closed. A glance showed him that there was nothing they could do for the landlord. Roker was beyond help.

'Our wolf decoy again,' Odell muttered bitterly. 'That's the second time we've been caught tonight. Let's get down and see what kind of an animal they've got in the cellar.'

Tommy Bourne followed at his chief's heels as they descended the stone steps to the cellar below. Fortunately there was an electric light fitted, and having found the switch they felt much more relieved. The howling began again, and on rounding a corner they saw, chained to the wall in a small alcove, a large Alsatian dog. It was pulling at the chain, but showed no signs of animosity towards the two men.

'Interesting.' Odell murmured as he hesitantly advanced towards the dog. 'This certainly isn't our mysterious wolf. See, it's dripping wet.' He bent down and examined the pool of water which had run off the beast's coat. 'Salt water, eh! This dog's been in the sea, Tommy. Another thing, it doesn't live here either. See the way it's straining to get away. I'd say, Tommy, that we've rather upset somebody's plans by being out there on the moors tonight.'

Odell paused, and drawing his pipe from his pocket he lit it. Drawing steadily on it, he remained lost in thought for some minutes. Finally he spoke.

'I'm going to take this dog out on to the moors and let him lead me to wherever he's going, Tommy,' he said. 'In the meantime I want you to take the car, and contact the police. I've an idea that we're up against something far more sinister than just a ghostly wolf!'

Odell set off across the moors, the Alsatian pulling at the chain by which the detective held it. On and on they went, the dog straining all the time as if in a frenzy to reach its destination. Then, for the third time that night, Odell heard the cry of a wolf. The Alsatian, on hearing it, gave a sudden pull, wrenched itself free of its captor and seconds later it was swallowed up in the night. Odell continued in the direction from which the cry had come. That was obviously where the dog was heading. Once more he grasped the revolver which rested in his pocket.

As he came over the brow of the hill, the detective saw a rambling old farmhouse nestling in the hollow below him. Lights were on, and there appeared to be a general air of activity about the place. He realised that the utmost caution was needed if he was going any closer to investigate.

Odell pressed himself close to the wall of the old stone barn. From where he was he could see into the kitchen of the house. Three or four rough looking men were gathered round the table, and appeared to be in deep conversation. Somewhere he could hear the barking of dogs, quite a few of them by the noise they were making. He crept closer in an attempt to hear what the men were saying. Too late his ears caught the sound of a soft footfall behind him and as he wheeled round, something descended on his head. Everything seemed to explode around him, and then he sank into oblivion.

* * *

Raymond Odell judged that he could not have been unconscious for very long. He discovered that he was bound hand and foot and was lying on the stone floor of the farmhouse kitchen. The men were still engaged in conversation. One of them turned around, noticing that their captive had regained consciousness.

'So, you've come to, have you, Mr Odell?' The detective recognised the speaker as none other than the ex-convict Marty Wiseman. 'Well, we've really got something in store for you, but as we've got an hour to kill before we can move from here, I may as well tell you what it's all about. Dead men tell no tales, so there's no harm in you knowing now.'

Raymond Odell listened intently, pushing everything else from his mind as the mystery unravelled. Wiseman went on talking. 'Drug smuggling, that's what we're up to, Mr. Raymond Odell. A launch slips into the bay below the moors, a couple of hundred yards out, and a signal is given.' He held up what appeared to be a hunting horn. 'This is the wolf howl. They've got one of these on the boat as well. When they give a blast our dogs swim out to the boat. Waterproof containers with heroin in them are strapped to their backs, and we give another wolf call to bring them back again. Anybody watching would never see the dogs slipping past them in the dark. And as for nosey-parkers,' he gave a laugh, 'we've got a special dog that doesn't go in the water. He's painted with luminous paint. Scares all the locals, and is trained to disappear through a gap up in the rocks on the hilltop. I believe even you lost sight of him there.'

He paused, but there was no response from the

detective, so he carried on.

'That swine Roker has been the trouble. He meant to blackmail us, and tonight he managed to capture one of the dogs and took it back to the 'Old Mariner'. I was on his trail, but then you butted in, and I had to fool you, pretending I was dead, while we drew you off with that wolf call. Anyway, I silenced Roker. It's a pity you had to carry on interfering though. Tonight's our last night. The drugs the dogs brought in are already on their way to London, and we're going to the continent in the launch, which is still out there. And so are you Mr. Odell, but only part of the way!'

Raymond Odell did not reply. The implication was only too clear. They intended to drop him overboard somewhere en route.

Half an hour later the party made its way across the moors towards the sea. Odell's legs had been freed to allow him to walk, but his hands were still bound tightly behind his back. They pushed him in front of them, forcing him to stumble along the rough terrain. There was one thought uppermost in Raymond Odell's mind. They had not mentioned Tommy Bourne. Perhaps in all the night's happenings they had overlooked the fact that his young assistant had even been with him.

At last the party reached the end of the moors. There was a narrow path down and Odell feared lest he might slip as he descended the path, which was more suitable for mountain goats.

Minutes later they were all standing on the beach.

'Can't see the boat,' Marty Wiseman muttered. 'He

should have moved in close by now.'

No sooner had he spoken than dark shapes materialised from behind the nearby rocks. There seemed to be men everywhere. Marty Wiseman, cursing fluently, tried to draw his automatic, but strong hands seized him, and rendered him helpless.

'This is the police,' a voice barked out. 'You're all under arrest.' A wave of relief flooded through Raymond Odell, and then he heard Tommy Bourne's voice at his side.

'Well done, Tommy,' he grunted, rubbing his sore wrists together, trying to restore the circulation. 'However did you manage to get here, though?'

'After I left you,' Tommy explained, 'I'd gone about a mile down the road when a car caught me up. He was going like the clappers, couldn't wait, overtook me on a bend, and piled his machine into the ditch. I'm afraid he put a dent in your car as well guvnor.' The young detective was relieved to hear his chief laugh, and went on, 'I pulled up to help him, but he was sparked out. I noticed that there were some canisters… guess what?'

'Heroin,' Raymond Odell replied. 'I know all about that, but go on.'

'I thought it would take too long rousing the local constabulary, so I used my mobile and got straight through to Richmond at the Yard. Fortunately, he was still there on special duty, and he soon got on the blower, and got these country coppers moving. The bloke who'd been knocked out in the car crash came round just as the police arrived. As soon as he realised the game was up he blew the gaff. I went with the police, and we arrested those smugglers in the launch as soon as they beached. All that remained was to wait for the rest of the gang to show up, and hope that you were still O.K. We figured that either you were still keeping watch or else they'd got you.'

'That's about it, sir,' the local police inspector approached the two detectives. 'I think we can safely say we've got the lot.'

'Good,' Raymond Odell replied, 'I think my assistant and I can do with some shut-eye now. We've had quite a night of it. By the way, Inspector,' he added as an afterthought. 'I'd like one of the wolf-calls these chaps were using, for my collection. I don't think the wolf will be howling on the moors anymore from now on.'

Hounds from Hades

(from Graveyard Rendezvous Summer 2009)

Creatures from hell exacted revenge
upon those who violated Nature's
domain.

The long, mournful howl shattered the stillness of the
cold winter's night, rose to a crescendo, and then died
away echoing for some time across the surrounding hills
until finally the silence rolled back. The brown owl
which had been hooting for some time beforehand was
now strangely silent. Field fares shifted uneasily in their
roost amidst the thick conifer plantations, and a vixen
which had been screaming her mating cry on a far off
crag slunk back to her earth beneath the rocks.

'Someone is going to die tonight,' Gwynne Evans,
the old hill-farmer, muttered as he came in from the
barn and closed the door behind him. His gnarled
fingers shot the bolt home. It was a long time since he

had locked up at night.

'The Black Dogs,' his grey-haired wife, bent almost double with rheumatics, stared into the blazing fire. 'Nigh on twenty years since we last heard 'em, the night that climber fell at Devil's Peak.'

'Aye,' Gwynne stared out of the window, pressing his face against the pane and attempting to shut out the reflection of the room. Sheep fields, silvery white with a thick hoar frost, stretched up until they met the black outline of the forest on the horizon. Forestry Commission plantations, closely planted trees which obscured the sunlight day after day, forbidding, refusing to yield the secrets of their gloomy depths. Did they hide the legendary spectral dogs, the hounds of hell, harbingers of doom? The legend stretched back to the Middle Ages. Anyone who saw the dogs died, and when their howling was heard death for somebody in the hills was certain. But for whom?

'Maybe it's just a stray dog,' the woman's voice trembled, destroying any conviction which her tone might have had. 'They do say that after old Maurice Jones passed away his dog took off and hasn't been seen since. It could be living up there in the forestry, gone half-wild.'

'No,' the farmer closed the curtains and turned back into the room. 'That weren't Gip. It was the Black Dogs. I guess we might as well go to bed. We'll know by morning, right enough, what it was all about... except them as the cry was for!'

Frank Hall, the head forester, stirred restlessly in his sleep. A long way off, a telephone was ringing. It was some minutes before its harsh jangling penetrated his slumbers sufficiently to make him aware that it was his phone down in the hall below. Cursing beneath his breath, still half-asleep, he swung his legs to the floor and groped for his dressing-gown on the chair beside the bed.

Panic hastened his wakening and the grimness of reality returned to him as he stumbled down the narrow stairs. It could be the hospital. It had to be at this hour. His wife. A terminal illness. The surgeons had done what they could. They had given her six months to live. Maybe the shock of the operation had cut her time.

His hand trembled as he lifted the receiver, and his vocal cords refused to function. It was a man's voice on the other end of the line, and it was several seconds before his dazed brain recognized it as that of Len Wright, his beat-forester.

'Poachers,' Len was breathless, 'up beyond the Devil's Peak. Using a Land Rover. After the deer.'

'Ok, Len,' he stammered, 'don't panic. We'll get 'em. Stand by. Give me a few minutes and I'll pick you up. And give the police a call, will you? If it's these same chaps who were raiding us last winter we could have our hands full.'

Frank Hall dressed hurriedly. Even at fifty years of age he moved quickly. He was as fit as he had been ten years ago. Deer poachers were all part of his routine. In fact, and he would not have admitted it to anybody else, they helped to break the monotony of life in these remote border hills. He needed something like this to help him get other things off his mind.

Wearing his heavy sheepskin jacket and corduroy

trousers he went outside and climbed into the Land Rover. The engine spluttered into life and then the wheels were bumping their way over uneven ground which separated the Head Forester's house from the lane. There was no need for the headlights. The moon had reached its zenith and hills and fields were portrayed in direct contrast of soft light and shadow. It was an ideal night for catching up with a gang of deer-poachers.

Len Wright was standing waiting in the road outside his cottage, his breath showing clearly in the freezing atmosphere.

'I got through to the police,' Len said as he clambered into the passenger seat. 'They'll get somebody out here as soon as they can.'

Frank Hall nodded and made a mental calculation. Fifteen miles, and allowing for communication and organization, the law was unlikely to show up for at least another half-hour. He turned off the hard road and took the steep unsurfaced forestry track which led towards Devil's Peak, the topmost crag in this range of hills. Even now he could see its outline in the moonlight, an escarpment scintillating above the forest, silhouetted against a black cloudless sky. There was no sign of the headlights which his assistant had reported seeing. Probably the poachers were on the small plateau behind the Peak, cruising slowly around, rifles at the ready in search of unsuspecting deer.

Ten minutes later, the ground levelled out and the Forester brought the vehicle to a standstill.

'Let's listen for a few minutes,' he found himself whispering. 'Maybe we'll get some idea of just where they are.'

The silence was almost overpowering.

Both men sensed its uncanniness, the absence of the nocturnal noises as though the whole of these hills had suddenly become a lifeless wilderness. Neither mentioned it to the other. Both found themselves wishing that they could seize upon some excuse for returning to the safety of their home.

Suddenly a barrage of shots rang out from up above them somewhere behind Devil's Peak. Rifles being fired as fast as fingers could squeeze the triggers. An engine was roaring as though being revved mercilessly in a low gear. And then the listening men heard the howling, a frenzied deep throated baying that drowned everything else like a thousand stag-hounds in full cry.

'My God!' Len Wright muttered. 'What is it?'

But Frank Hall did not reply. His face deathly white, he was staring up towards the Peak, throat dry, vocal cords refusing to function again. He knew the legend. Until now he had scoffed at the tale, but this time there was no logical explanation. And not for a thousand pounds would he have driven any further up that track.

The two watching men saw the Land Rover come into view, its twin headlights piercing the darker shadow of Devil's Peak, elevating as the vehicle scaled a sharp incline, then dipping and levelling as it found flat ground again. It was surely out control. Vivid flashes denoted more rifle fire but the reports were lost in the baying which drowned everything else.

The watching foresters had an unrestricted view of the careering Land Rover, it's crazy course back and forth on the plateau of shale and heather, never slowing, seemingly trying to turn but always reverting to its original direction which led directly to the precipice below the Peak.

More firing. Yet there was no sign of any other form of life. Sheer madness, a gang of hardened poachers driving towards certain death whilst raking the area at their rear with a constant hail of bullets. The Land Rover checked momentarily as though the driver had braked sharply and then jerked forward, picking up speed rapidly, this time heading straight for the edge of the cliff.

'They're going over!' Len Wright screamed.

Frank Hall's nails bit deeply into the palms of his hands as he saw the vehicle shoot out into space and seem to hover like some earth-orbiting craft, then plunge downwards to the forested ravine below. The canine baying reached its peak and then died away. Silence, the atmosphere heavy with an aura of evil, the cold more intense than ever. A reddish glow spread up into the night sky and the two forestry men could hear the crackling of flames. The fire from the smashed and blazing Land Rover was spreading through the thickets as though trying to erase the memories of this very night; pillars of smoke rising up into the sky in the beginnings of a forest fire that no living man could check, an inferno that seemed to have come from Hades itself.

The following day was well advanced before Frank Hall drove up on the plateau that adjoined Devil's Peak. Below him the blaze raged relentlessly, driving back the team of fire-fighters under the control of Len Wright.

The Head Forester left his Land Rover and walked across the open space of level ground. Flakes of burning debris floated down around him like black snowflakes but he ignored them, his keen grey eyes scanning the ground in front of him.

After some searching he managed to find the tyre tracks which he sought, imprinted on the barren surface, twisting crazily this way and that. Then his expression hardened and his lips tightened into a thin bloodless line. Deer spoor he was familiar with, the churning hoof marks of a passing herd, but these huge paw-prints had not been made by any passing herd of fallow or sika. They were barely discernible on the rocky ground, a scuffing of the soil here and there, more distinct around the odd boggy patch. But there was no mistaking the footprint of a dog, a hound of immense proportions, creatures that had been invisible to the watching mortals yet seen in terrifying clarity by those whom the pack pursued.

Frank Hall nodded to himself and began to retrace his steps. It was no concern of his. The hounds had come from hell and now they had returned there in accordance with the legend. Those who had violated the laws of nature had paid the ultimate penalty. When Black Dogs were heard, someone died. The Head Forester had witnessed a brand of justice meted out by the spectral hounds, to those poachers who had violated the law of these hills. It was the law of this hill country dating back to time immemorial, and it would always be so.

Guy N. Smith

I Couldn't Care Less

(from Graveyard Rendezvous 40)

Guy N. Smith

Malcolm Palmer could not remember how long he had been in the condemned cell. Sometimes he thought it was only since yesterday, other times it seemed years. They had returned capital punishment to Britain, he didn't know when and he wasn't really interested. All he knew was that one of the mornings they would come for him, lead him down to the execution chamber and that would be that. Finis!

He had not appealed against his sentence. Or rather, if his lawyer had done so then he had not informed Malcolm. In fact, Malcolm did not mind dying at all because there was nothing left to live for now that Paula was gone. They had found him guilty of her murder and that hurt a lot. But, on reflection, he had had plenty of time to think about it, his wife would know that he had not killed

her. Soon they would be together. He couldn't wait to join her; he just wished that he knew when it would be.

He went over it all again in his tortured mind, the shock and the tragedy, the grief that had blinded him to all else. He had been shaving in the bathroom that fateful morning when he had heard Paula going downstairs. If she had walked slowly, carefully, like he was always telling her to do, then she would still be alive today and he would not be cooped up in this pokey little cell waiting to die. But Paula was fifteen years younger than himself and she did everything at teenage speed.

Instead of holding on to the banister, she ran downstairs. Because the phone was ringing in the hall.

'Let 'em bloody well wait!' he had shouted after her.

Too late! He heard her trip. She gave a kind of startled squeal and then he heard her going all the way down the steep flight. Bump-bump-bumpety-bump. Crash!

Oh, God! He almost yelled his anguish aloud just at the very memory. He had rushed out of the bathroom, stared in horror at the petite form lying at an unnatural angle on the hall floor, her head twisted to one side. Sitting in his cell now it all came back to him just as though it had happened this very minute. Again. He had rushed downstairs, his face still lathered in shaving foam, and tried to pick her up. Her head had lolled; she had stared up at him with sightless eyes.

No, you're not dead, Paula. Please don't die. Everything's going to be fine.

He had carried her through to the settee in the lounge, laid her there and gone and made her a strong cup of tea with three sugars. 'Drink your tea, Paula, you'll feel better then. Then we'll go downtown and I'll buy you that dress you wanted.'

She didn't drink her tea. She never moved again. He stayed and comforted her for three whole days; the police said it was a week because she had started to smell when they finally came for her.

Paula went to the mortuary and Malcolm was taken to the police station. They asked him question after question but he wasn't able to tell them much because he couldn't remember. 'All right, I kept her for a week, then. I was hoping she'd get better.'

'I'm afraid we're going to have to charge you, Malcolm Palmer.'

Now Paula was dead, it didn't matter. He gave up telling them that she'd fallen downstairs, they didn't believe him anyway.

'Just do what you want with me, I couldn't care less…couldn't care less…'

He remembered something his father told him, wagging a stern finger at him every time he said that when he was a small boy. '*Don't care* was hanged.' Even in boyhood Malcolm had queried that silly statement. They didn't hang people for not caring.

Well, apparently they did.

Malcolm's brain had switched off, nothing registered with him because it didn't matter any longer. They were going to hang him, drop him down through the trap door and either his neck would be dislocated or else he would die from strangulation.

I couldn't care less.

It was strange how morbid subjects like hanging fascinated small boys. When Malcolm was six his father had taken him to a church garden fete, one of the sideshows had been a miniature gallows. It cost a penny to go into the tent and when the tent was full the man tied the flap. The show lasted about two seconds, the tiny figure, a black hood over its head, dropped down though the trap door and you could just see its feet swinging, twisting one way then the other.

Everybody out. Next please! Malcolm had not got any further than that tent; he'd spent the whole shilling which his father had given him in there. Twelve hangings. Well thirteen, actually because the man let him watch one free as he was a regular customer!

A few years later he had read an article in the newspaper about hanging – "What

Really Happens." Sometimes, when the hangman miscalculated his weights and measures, the victim's head came off. On one occasion they had had to pull the guy back up and hang him again because they'd made a cock-up. Malcolm wondered if it was any different these days. He couldn't care less.

*   *   *

They had drugged him, he guessed that much. Slipped something in his tea, doubtless. His vision was distorted as he stumbled out of the cell and along the corridor. He knew what they were doing, all right. The rope was rough against his neck; chafed it. They didn't need to blindfold him because he couldn't see, anyway. Nobody spoke, thank God!

They weren't very expert, fumbling about, trying to get the noose right. In the end they managed it and pulled it tight. *Good, and I hope my bloody head comes off, makes a right mess for you to clean up.*

Frankly I could care less so you'd better get on with it and hang me.

* * *

The coroner's court wasn't even a sombre affair. Merely a formality because the law demanded it. There were neither friends nor relatives present because the deceased had neither. Just police and a local press reporter. It might make a paragraph in Friday's Journal, depending upon how much there was to cover at the parish council meetings.

The coroner cleared his throat. He had an annoying habit of speaking quickly in a soft voice; those within the room leaned forward in an attempt to catch what he said. If it was anything interesting. Today nobody appeared interested. The clock on the wall said five minutes to one. Everybody present had their minds on lunch. Including the coroner himself.

The reporter scribbled indecipherable shorthand, often he could not read it himself when he got back to the office. Today it didn't matter much, anyway.

'Malcolm Palmer, late of…' The reporter missed the address. 'Had been undergoing psychiatric treatment but refused it a month ago. Devastated by the death of his wife… An accident but he kept the body at home for a week… charged with failing to report a death. He collapsed in court and was referred for the afore-mentioned treatment. He became a recluse; the neighbours had not seen him for weeks. Suffered from depression and delusions…'

A rustle of papers; the clock on the wall said two

minutes to one, there wasn't much time left. The coroner spoke even faster. Nobody was listening. 'Found hanged from the stair banisters. Verdict: suicide whilst the balance of the mind was disturbed.'

Nobody could have cared less.

Sabat: The Robber's Grave

(additional story)

Guy N. Smith

1821

The small courtroom at Welshpool was crowded, mostly with sensation seekers anticipating a death sentence. Judge Winderholme's lined features wore an expression that could only be termed as boredom. This trial had lasted for most of the day when he could have pronounced a guilty verdict hours ago. Yet he was compelled to listen to the witnesses' somewhat garbled evidence against the accused. He stifled a yawn. Just another ten minutes would bring it to a conclusion. His fingers toyed with the black cap on his knee.

In the dock, head bowed, stood John Davies, a plasterer and slaterer, a resident of Montgomery. He was accused of assaulting William Jones, a labourer, and robbing him of a watch worth all of fifty shillings. Both witnesses, Walter Hughes and William Lewis had not actually been present at the assault but had heard Jones's cries for help and upon going to his aid had glimpsed Davies in the distance. They had also come upon the missing watch lying on a path, the one upon which Davies had departed the scene.

Davies denied assault and theft which was only to be expected. Jones had identified the watch as being the one stolen from him. The judge stifled another yawn; it was a clear cut case in his view, otherwise this trial might well go on for several more hours.

'I am innocent,' Davies's voice trembled. 'I never touched William Jones nor stole his watch. It is a frame up because of a previous disagreement I had with these liars!'

'Silence!' The judge unravelled the square of black cloth and draped it over his balding head. 'John Davies, this court finds you guilty of assault and theft. Hence, I sentence you to be hanged by the neck until you are dead and may the Lord have mercy upon your soul.'

A small crowd had gathered in Montgomery for the public execution, an exciting event in this sleepy Welsh town. Davies stood upon the gallows and the hangman draped the loop of rope around the doomed man's neck. Dark clouds gathered in the sky overhead and a bolt of lightning lit up the grim scene below. Thunder crashed and a heavy downpour began.

Suddenly John Davies straightened up, addressed the spectators in defiant tones.

'I go to my grave an innocent man, wrongly executed for a crime which I did not commit. Let this wrongful act lie upon all your consciences and may God prevent grass from growing upon my grave as a sign of my innocence.'

Another crash of thunder drowned the excited chattering of the crowd as the body of John Davies dropped and swung.

His grave was situated on the far side of the parish cemetery well clear of the rows of tombstones. It was marked by a basic wooden crucifix simply carved "The Robber's Grave." As the years passed, there was no sign of growth upon the ground above his burial site. It was muttered with no small amount of awe by local inhabitants that this in itself was proof that an innocent man had paid the supreme penalty upon the lying by so-called witnesses to a crime which had never taken place.

2018

Mark Sabat was tall and very agile for one in his mid to late sixties, his hair and moustache still black apart from a few wisps of grey. His long career as a private detective who investigated cases which had an occult implication was drawing to a close. Retirement beckoned, much to the disappointment of his few police associates who had held him in esteem for many years. There were others who doubted his unique findings and were glad that he would no longer be called upon to investigate crimes which had inexplicable backgrounds.

Throughout the years he had been fighting against the soul of his evil brother, Quentin, who had somehow infiltrated his own inner self. Many battles between the two had ensued but, much to his relief, Quentin had been silent recently. Mark feared, though, that the latter had not departed his own inner self forever. He was still haunted in his sleep by the other's maniacal mocking laughter.

Mark's London apartment was now on the market and was creating interest but so far there was no firm buyer. It seemed that everybody had a property to sell before they could invest in a new home.

Breakfast was finished and he was contemplating a day of leisure, maybe a visit to the British Museum, when the telephone shrilled.

'Hello, Sabat,' a familiar voice on the other end which he recognised as that of Inspector McCaulay of Scotland Yard, a long-time associate whom he had worked with on several occasions over the years.

Sabat groaned inwardly, the last thing he wanted at this stage of his career with retirement in prospect was a call from the Yard.

'McCaulay,' he lowered himself into a chair. 'Much as I enjoy talking to you I'm on the verge of retirement. The last thing I need is an investigation.'

'Well, I'd appreciate your opinion, anyway, Sabat. You know how much I value it.' Flattery was always a good starting point.

'I'd be happy to oblige but I really don't want another case. As you know, retirement beckons and I'm really looking forward to it.'

'Sure, I appreciate that. However I have had a phone call from a colleague of mine, Superintendent Jackson, of the Powys police force in Wales. We once worked together. Now he's got a mystery on his hands and he's heard of you and asked if I could have a chat with you.

On the face of it occult forces are at large in Montgomery.'

Oh, Christ, here we go! Sabat suppressed a groan.

'There's been a murder up in Wales. The body was found in Montgomery churchyard. The victim, a guy in his late fifties, had been strangled. What he was doing wandering around a rural graveyard after dark is something of a mystery. The force used was so great that his neck had been completely snapped!'

'These days there's usually more than one murder every day,' Sabat replied. 'So why should you be interested in one up in rural Wales?'

'There's more to it than that, Sabat. Back in the mid-nineteenth century a local guy was apprehended in that same churchyard by a couple of chaps who claimed he had stolen a watch from them. The evidence was weak but he was found guilty and hanged publicly. On the gallows he swore his innocence and announced that to support his claim no grass or undergrowth would grow on his grave. And oddly that was the case, proof enough for superstitious locals until fairly recently weeds began to sprout there. Folks avoided the grave on the grounds that Davies was no longer down there and he was out and about. Nobody would venture near the site except curious holidaymakers who had read about the legend. Now we come to the weird bit and I wouldn't even mention it except to yourself.'

'Go on,' Sabat was curious.

'The guy who was murdered was a descendant of William Jones whom it is believed produced two false witnesses to ensure that Davies was found guilty. Now there's rumours that Davies has risen from his grave to seek revenge. Of course the police dismiss this theory as rubbish. Some of the locals have applied to the Church for permission to exhume Davies's remains, or, at least, find out if they are still down there. Needless to say their request has been refused.'

Sabat pursed his lips. His past experience of his investigations had him keeping an open mind at this stage.

And then somewhere deep within himself he heard a sneer. Quentin was stirring again after a lengthy absence. Because he knew something about this strange business far from here. Mark tensed. The silence returned.

'What d'you want me to do about the Robber's Grave, then McCaulay?'

'I was wondering,' the other's hesitancy was unmistakable, 'if you would fancy a trip up to Montgomery. Incognito, of course. If anybody can find out what's going on up there, it's you. Maybe a break from the metropolis would do you good.'

Sabat sighed. Maybe it would lead to a final encounter with Quentin, allow him to see out his final years in peace.

'All right,' he added after a pause. 'I'll take a trip up there and have a mooch around. I can't promise more than that.'

'Thanks,' there was a note of relief in the other's voice. 'It's out of my area but you and I have conducted numerous weird investigations. I could ignore it but Superintendent Jackson feels there's more to this business than meets the eye. Anyway, I owe him a personal favour. So I'll leave it all up to you and hope to hear from you in due course.'

Sabat arrived in Montgomery a few days later and booked into an hotel. Such a charming town, was his first impression. There was nothing in the way of nocturnal rowdiness here at night, mostly the younger generation travelled to either Newtown or Welshpool for their drinking, so the hotel receptionist informed him. 'You will enjoy a really peaceful few days here, sir.'

Dusk was creeping in on a calm, late autumn evening when he set out for the churchyard. The streets were empty, the town itself was deserted apart from a couple of locals returning from the late-opening shop. It couldn't be better for his purpose, he reflected, as he entered the churchyard. There was a full moon, its wan light penetrating the overhanging branches of the tall trees. He had no need of his torch for which he was grateful. The last thing he wanted was to advertise his presence in these holy grounds.

Suspended from his neck was the silver crucifix which he always wore on such investigations. On more than one occasion it had kept Quentin at bay. He had not, though, brought his revolver loaded with silver bullets. It could have been problematic if for any reason the police became involved. Anyway, he consoled himself, this was just a brief investigation to oblige an old colleague.

He came upon a sign indicating that the "Robber's Grave" was somewhere to the left of the main pathway. There was no problem finding it, a heap of soil and weeks where there should have been level ground, a crude wooden crucifix lying atop it, designating

"Robbers Grave." *Had somebody dug down to exhume the remnants of the corpse or else had it risen by itself?*

'Jesus Christ!' Sabat muttered. He had no need of his torch for a ray of moonlight lit up the digging. *Then somewhere within himself he heard sneering laughter. Most certainly this was Quentin's evil work.*

Sabat bent, lifted up the crude cross. It was lightweight, doubtless a replacement for the original which had rotted over the years. Maybe some local had put it there, an apology from the ancestors of those who had been responsible for the injustice.

Yet weeds had established themselves in recent times, contrary to Davies' statement from the gallows that the soil would reject natural growth as proof of his innocence.

Could it be that his skeleton no longer lay buried down there and he had risen from his burial place, aided by Quentin Sabat? An icy shiver trickled down Mark's spine and even as he looked around him he sensed his brother sneering within him.

Up ahead something moved, hidden in the shadows, like somebody was treading through the undergrowth, uncertain of their balance on the uneven ground. Sabat froze, clenched the crucifix with one hand, his silver neckpiece with the other.

'Prepare to meet the one you are seeking, Mark. Prepare to join him. The dead shall walk again!'

Suddenly a figure moved out into the moonlight, Sabat gasped aloud at that which he saw. The features were near skeletal, strips of flesh peeling from the head; holes where there should have been eyes, glowing. Mucus stringing from the place where once flesh had covered a nose. A snarling toothless mouth agape, drool oozing down the chin. The body was bent and stooped, rotting clothing hanging from it in strips. The bare feet struggled for balance. Undoubtedly this was John Davies, a rusted carving knife clutched in a bony hand, raised from his final resting place by Quentin Sabat and seeking revenge upon those who had sent an innocent man to the gallows.

Sabat wished fervently that he had been carrying his revolver. One silver bullet would have ended the other's zombie existence. He held up his silver crucifix but Davies only advanced another couple of unsteady steps, his knife raised. Angry grunts came from the slobbering mouth. Somewhere Quentin was sneering.

Sabat gripped his crucifix, the only weapon which he possessed. They were now face to face, Davies raising his knife, preparing to deliver a fatal blow. Instinctively Sabat wielded that frail cross, struck with every ounce of strength which he could muster. It found its mark, shattered and splintered on that peeling skull.

An inhuman scream of agony rent the night air. Davies crumpled to the ground, not so much as a twitch from the remnants of his splayed body. Somewhere Quentin was cursing but Mark ignored him, leaning against a tree trunk for support.

Now all he had to do was to return John Davies to his last resting place. A search around the area of the disturbed grave revealed a spade, obviously the one which Quentin had used for the exhumation, doubtless stolen from somewhere. Fortunately the soil was soft from its previous disturbance. Sweat soaked his shirt as he dug and scooped until the cavity was large enough for the pathetic jumble of bones. He tossed the broken crucifix in before scraping back the earth and levelling it.

Quentin was silent, subdued in defeat once again.

'May you rest in peace, John Davies,' Sabat made the sign of the cross and walked away, carrying the spade. He would dispose of it somewhere, leaving behind him another mystery for the superstitious locals.

Grass had grown on The Robber's Grave but now it was gone. Tomorrow he would call McCaulay. Doubtless this night's events would remain a secret between the two of them; nobody would believe them, anyway, and the search for the murderer would remain on file for evermore.

It was best left that way, Mark Sabat concluded. Only he and McCaulay would know the true facts and the latter would not be revealing them. Right now Mark's forthcoming retirement was more appealing than ever.

Gallery

The following pages show the original covers to the Graveyard Rendezvous that featured the stories within this collection.

Graveyard Rendezvous No. 1 featured *Shooting on the Moss*.

Graveyard Rendezvous No. 2 featured *The Ghouls*.

Graveyard Rendezvous No. 4 featured *The Lurkers*.

Graveyard Rendezvous No. 6 featured *The Executioner*.

Graveyard Rendezvous No. 9 featured *Cannibal Island*.

Graveyard Rendezvous No. 14 featured *Mr. Strange's Christmas Dream.*

Graveyard Rendezvous No. 16 featured *The Case of the Ostrich Slasher.*

£3.50

LIONEL FANTHORPE
SPECIAL ISSUE

Member of:
NAFC

No.
16

The Guy N. Smith Fanzine

Guy N. Smith

Graveyard Rendezvous No. 19 featured *The Werewolf Legend.*

Graveyard Rendezvous No. 35 featured *The Howling on the Moors.*

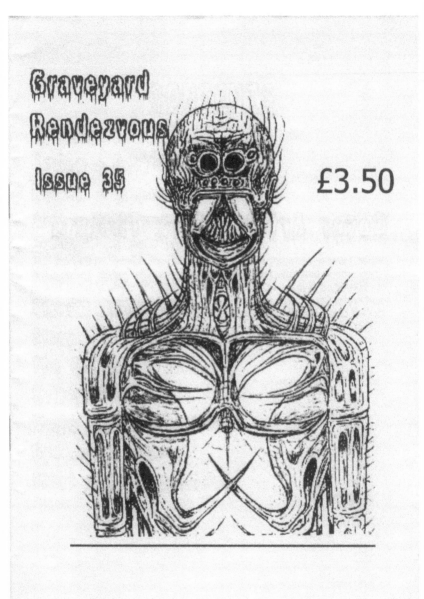

Graveyard Rendezvous Summer 2009 featured *Hounds from Hades.*

Graveyard Rendezvous No. 40 featured *I Couldn't Care Less*.

Graveyard Rendezvous 40
Autumn Issue 2011

£3.50

ABOUT THE AUTHOR

Guy N. Smith has been a best-selling author for over 40 years. He has written over 70 horror novels since 1975 as well as numerous short stories in the genre. He continues to publish books every year.

Find out more at www.guynsmith.com

Also from the Sinister Horror Company

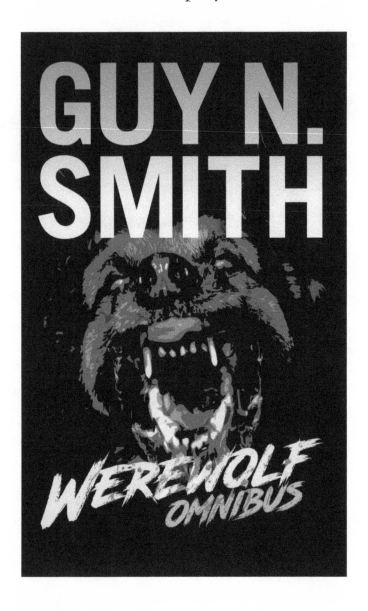

Guy N. Smith's
Werewolf Omnibus

Are werewolves simply folklore or have they existed at some stage in the distant past?

Lycanthropy is known to be a mental condition where the sufferer believes himself to be a wolf and embarks upon a psychotic rampage. So perhaps there's some truth in the age-old legends.

The Black Hill in South Shropshire is a dark forest where legend becomes reality. As well as werewolves seeking human prey, the hills hold tales of the black dogs. A sighting of these spectral canines is a harbinger of death.

Gordon Hall, the sporting tenant, finds himself caught up in these ancient horrors and is determined to destroy them once and for all.

Both his life and his soul are at risk.

Werewolf Omnibus collects together three vintage novels from the master of pulp horror, Guy N. Smith: Werewolf By Moonlight (1974), Return Of The Werewolf (1977) and The Son Of The Werewolf (1978), alongside a new short story, Spawn Of The Werewolf.

Also from the Sinister Horror Company

HORROR LURKED IN THE MAZE OF CLIFF CAVES WHERE A
NEW GENERATION OF GIANT CRABS WERE BREEDING.

THE CHARNEL CAVES

GUY N. SMITH

The Charnel Caves: A Crabs Novel

Horror lurked in the maze of cliff caves where a new generation of giant crabs were breeding.

In 1975 an army of gigantic crabs, the result of an underwater nuclear experiment, attacked the Welsh coastline.

The battle was bloody, many lives were lost until the crustacean invaders were defeated.

Over the ensuing years they turned up in the oceans of the World with further terrible slaughter of humans. Finally, though, it was believed that these monsters from the deep had been eradicated. Only memories of their invasions of land remained with the older inhabitants, tales of their depredations on mankind were whispered but often ridiculed by the modern generations.

Until a few of the survivors returned to the Welsh coast and began breeding secretly in a maze of caverns beneath the cliffs, preparing for a further attack on mankind.

Also from the Sinister Horror
Company

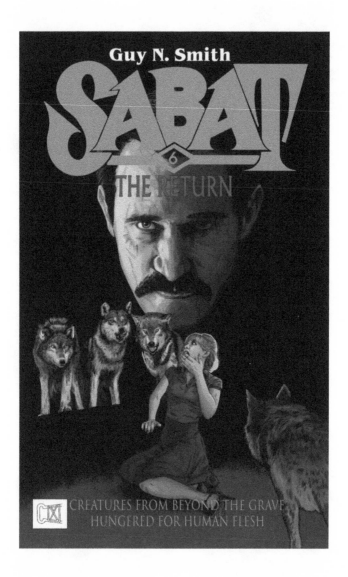

The Charnel Caves: A Crabs Novel

Creatures for, beyond the grave hungered for human flesh.

Mark Sabat, ex-priest, SAS-trained killer, exorcist, had been a man with a dreadful mission for most of his life. His evil brother, Quentin, had chosen the Left Hand Path and his soul had haunted Mark.

Finally, Quentin had been destroyed but now Mark faces another enemy, master criminal The Reaper who is also one of Satan's disciples. The Reaper, following his escape from prison, is bent on revenge on G. N. Strong, the private detective who had been instrumental in his capture.

Sabat's role is to protect Strong from a deadly foe who has supernatural powers.

His enemy is the eternal principle of evil made flesh.

The Black Room Manuscripts Volume Three

Guy N. Smith features in *The Black Room Manuscripts Volume Three* with his short story **Toad In The Hole**.

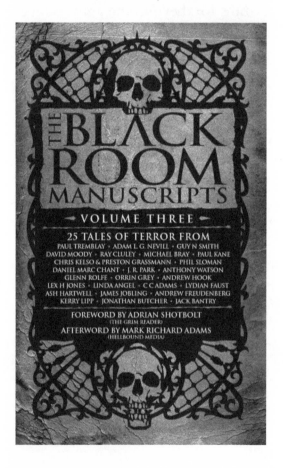

All profits made the sale of this book go to the charity Shelter.

The Black Room Manuscripts Volume Three

SINISTER
HORROR
COMPANY

Some words are born in shadows.

Some tales told only in whispers.

Under the paper thin veneer of our sanity is a world that exists. Hidden just beyond, in plain sight, waiting to consume you should you dare stray from the street-lit paths that sedate our fears.

For centuries the Black Room has stored stories of these encounters, suppressing the knowledge of the rarely seen. Protecting the civilised world from its own dark realities.

The door to the Black Room has once again swung open to unleash twenty five masterful tales of the macabre from the twisted minds of a new breed of horror author.

The Black Room holds many secrets.

Dare you enter…for a third time?

Guy N. Smith Illustrated Bibliography

"The sheer effort and dedication that's gone into creating this unbelievably comprehensive bibliography is breath-taking." – DLS Reviews

The complete(ish) guide to collecting the works of Guy N. Smith.

A journey into collecting the works of prolific author Guy Newman Smith. The book covers all genres of the Great Scribbler's writing and contains over 950 pictures and useful details to assist any would-be collector.

Guy N. Smith Illustrated Bibliography

The author has endeavoured to list and visually represent, through over 950 colour pictures, the vast catalogue of output from Guy N. Smith's 65+ years in print; from the early stories he had published in the Tettenhall Observer and Advertiser paper as a teenager through to the present day. A career that crosses fiction and non-fiction and has covered almost all possible genres along the way, from Self-Sufficiency to Westerns, via Countryside and Glamour magazines of the 70s, all in addition to the numerous horror and thriller titles he is better known for.

Content includes Fiction (all imprints/editions inc. non UK) and Non-Fiction Categories: Horror, Thriller, Countryside and Children's Novels, Omnibus Collections, Chapbooks, Graphic Novels, Anthologies, Fanzines, Booklets, Magazines (70s adult Glamour, Country Sport, Game-keeping, Horror etc.), Periodicals and Newspapers.

The book also contains an original Guy N. Smith short story 'The Beast in the Cage' along with humorous insight into the levels of collecting Guy N. Smith's works in 'The Completist- A Cautionary Tale' by author Shane P.D Agnew.

A4 Size, 950+ colour pictures, 341 pages.

Available via Amazon.

The Sinister Horror Company is an independent UK publisher of genre fiction. Their mission a simple one – to write, publish and launch innovative and exciting genre fiction by themselves and others.

For further information on the Sinister Horror Company visit:

SinisterHorrorCompany.com
Facebook.com/sinisterhorrorcompany
Twitter @SinisterHC

SINISTERHORRORCOMPANY.COM

CPSIA information can be obtained
at www.ICGtesting.com
Printed in the USA
BVHW071656190123
656617BV00007B/682

9 781912 578245